OUT OF PRINT

OUT OF PRINT

A Novel

JOHN W. FRYE

credo
house publishers

To Margaret,
my mother, who introduced me
to the wonder of the Bible

Out of Print

Copyright © 2007 by John W. Frye

All rights reserved.

Published in the United States by Credo House Publishers,
a division of Credo Communications, LLC, Grand Rapids, Michigan.
www.credocommunications.net

To respond to the message of this book, for more information about the author's ministry, and for details on how to order additional copies of *Out of Print*, please contact us at

John W. Frye
4637 Breckenridge NE
Grand Rapids, MI 49525

Email: jfrye25@comcast.net

World Wide Web: www.jesustheradicalpastor.blogspot.com

ISBN: 978-0-9787620-7-0

Editor: Moriah Sharp
Cover design: Grey Matter Group
Author image: Marie Clark Photography
Interior design and composition: Sharon VanLoozenoord

Scripture is taken from the HOLY BIBLE, NEW INTERNATIONAL VERSION®. NIV®. Copyright © 1973, 1978, 1984 by International Bible Society. Used by permission of Zondervan. All rights reserved.

Printed in the United States of America

10 9 8 7 6 5 4 3 2 1

First Edition

The interested reader will find an author's afterword at the back of the book, as well as acknowledgements and an afterword by Scot McKnight, Karl A. Olsson Professor in Religious Studies at North Park University.

Contents

Prologue
xi

1
UNTHINKABLE
1

2
UNEXPLAINABLE
19

3
UNSTOPPABLE
39

4
UNSURPASSABLE
73

Epilogue
101

Author's Afterword
103

Afterword by Scot McKnight
105

Acknowledgments
107

Prologue

Dating near AD 150, the Rylands Papyrus is one of the earliest manuscript fragments of the New Testament Gospel of John. The fragment, known as P52, records John 18:31–33 and 18:37–38.

At 2:37 a.m. on September 15 in the John Rylands Library in Manchester, England, the ancient Greek letters disappeared from P52.

Alexander Morrow, the museum director, and Stanley Will, the chief of security, ordered a complete and vigorous investigation. They were stunned not only by this alarming incident, but even more by the results of the thorough investigation. Not a hint of evidence was detected suggesting any form of criminal activity.

"The days are coming," declares the Sovereign LORD,
*"when I will send a famine through the land—
not a famine of food or a thirst for water,
but a famine of hearing the words of the LORD."*

AMOS 8:11

1

UNTHINKABLE

SEPTEMBER 20

An early morning misty fog blanketed the neighborhood like a large, cozy, comforter, inviting everyone to snuggle down in bed for a little more sleep. But Ben Cook had not been persuaded to postpone the start to his day. As he walked to the end of his driveway to retrieve his newspaper, he gazed around in the gentle dawn, enjoying the quiet, cool tranquility of his suburban street. River Valley was a fairly new development on the northeastern edge of Grand Rivers, Michigan, a metropolitan area of 750,000 people. It had a good school system and several Bible teaching churches. Knowing they hoped to start a family soon, Ben and his wife, Anne, were glad to find a home in such a good neighborhood when they relocated to the area two years ago.

Coffee mug in hand, Ben settled into his reading chair and scanned the major headlines—Suicide Bomber Kills 15 in Tel Aviv Market, River Valley High Losing Streak Continues, Vanishing Papyrus Baffles Scholars.

"Looks like all the news today is either bad or boring." Ben set the paper aside and reached for his New Testament. "On second thought, maybe I'll start off with some good news first, and then face the world."

Shortly after Ben and Anne moved to River Valley, they had joined Three Rivers Community Church. Launched into being by the large, well-known Grace Church, Three Rivers had attracted a variety of people from the surrounding developments in the five years since it first began. Ben and Anne liked the pastor and enjoyed the friendships they had established over the last two years. As part of a men's accountability group there, Ben had recently been challenged to make a commitment to read the Bible daily. He was told, among other things, that it would be a great help in becoming a good husband and father. Ben had decided to start out with the Gospel of John, remembering a sermon series that Steve Roberts, pastor at Three Rivers, had preached a year before on that Gospel. Those sermons had developed within Ben a deeper devotion to Jesus, as well as an admiration for the Apostle John's account. He was especially looking forward to this morning's reading. John chapter 8 presented the account of the woman caught in the act of adultery. Her life was in danger. Jesus masterfully saved her life from ruthless religious leaders bent on stoning her to death. Ben recalled the riveting sermon Steve had preached on this passage and was anxious to relive the tension and wonder of the story.

Ben opened his Bible to the place he had marked the day before. He saw the chapter number 8 and verse numbers, but otherwise the page was blank. *That's strange,* he thought. Ben blinked his eyes several times thinking his sight was failing. He turned to the next page. No words appeared there either. He quickly flipped forward through the pages, then backward until he came to the Gospel of Luke. The pages of John's Gospel were blank.

Ben's heart began to race. He scanned quickly through John again. He felt an ache grip him in the pit of his stomach. *What's going on here!*

In a cold sweat, he frantically rustled here and there through all the books of his Bible. Everywhere he turned he was greeted with the reassuring sight of printed pages. There was Psalms. Hebrews. Jonah. Ephesians. Isaiah. The Gospel of Luke was all there. And the book of Acts was right where it should be. But John was nowhere to be seen. This just couldn't be; he had read from this same Bible the previous morning.

Ben stared at the blank cavern where John should have been, trying to get a grip on what was happening. His heart was pounding. "I read John 7 yesterday," he heard himself saying. "It was right here." He moved his fingers down the empty pages and noticed that he was trembling. *What's happened to the words in the Gospel of John? They've vanished into thin air.*

A soft clattering sound came from the kitchen. His wife had roused herself out of the cozy embrace of the warm bed, and was pouring herself a cup of Cook's Special Blend.

"Anne, Anne! Come here! John's missing!" he yelled.

"What happened?" Anne shuffled into the room, with obvious concern lining her tired face. "Who's missing?"

"Not who, *what*. The Gospel of John is not in my Bible!"

"Oh," Anne let out a relieved sigh, and nestled herself in the corner of the couch closest to Ben. "I thought you were talking about some poor little missing child you'd read about in the paper or something."

The paper. Hadn't one of the headlines said something about some vanishing words off of some old papyrus? Ben grabbed the paper and hunted for the article that he had only minutes before thought boring.

"So, some pages fell out from your Bible?" Anne continued after a sip of coffee. "Well, have you checked under your chair? That's where anything important tends to show up."

"No, Anne. The pages are there, it's the words that are gone. And look at this—in the paper—some words from the Gospel of John disappeared from some old piece of papyrus—"

He folded the paper open to the story and handed it to her.

ANCIENT PAPYRUS PUZZLES SCHOLARS

Anne looked up at Ben and saw her own fear and confusion mirrored in his eyes.

"Ben, w-what's going on?"

"I don't know . . ." Ben faded off. "Go get your Bible, Anne. Quick! And turn to John 8. Hurry! See if it's there."

Anne ran to the bedroom, grabbed her Bible from the nightstand and was shuffling through to find John's Gospel as she raced back to Ben.

"Here it i-i-is—isn't," she said to Ben with a catch in her throat. "There are no words on my pages either. The Gospel of John is gone."

Ben's eyes were wide with stunned confusion. "Oh, my God."

"What's happening, Ben? What's going on?"

"I don't know, Anne, I just don't know. I think we had better call Steve."

● ● ●

If that airplane were a car, I'd call it an old jalopy, Hank Myers mused. As he and his wife, Karla, watched, the small four-seat Cessna rumbled down the grassy airstrip and climbed into the air, just clearing the trees in the distance. Jim Samsa, the missionary aviation pilot and their good friend and lifeline to the outside world, banked the plane to the left. Jim had brought them some paper supplies, a new belt for a generator, and some topical medicine for a young boy with an infected cut on his foot. Jim also could always be counted on to bring newsy, almost gossipy, reports about other missionaries who lived and worked in the field office in the compound in Nabire.

Hank and Karla waited until the drone of the engine faded to silence and the plane disappeared in the huge air space of the valley. Only then did they turn to walk hand in hand up the short inclined path to their home—a rough bungalow in the mountain jungle area in the interior of Irian Jaya. It was just the two of them in their home now as Tracy, their sixteen-year-old daughter, was away at school in the States living with Karla's sister's family.

Six years ago, Hank and Karla came to live among the Vahudati and put their ancient tribal dialect into written form. They quickly fell in love with the Vahudati, a people group of almost four thousand, as they listened intently to the language sounds, produced an alphabetic/syllabic language system, and worked patiently and lovingly to teach the Vahudati to read and write their own language. A significant part of their mission work, their vocational dream come true, was to translate the good news of Jesus Christ in the Vahudati language. For the past three and a half years they had been laboring to translate the Gospel of John into Vahudati with the help of Seigi, an extremely gifted Vahudati man who had become passably fluent in English from spending several years in a large coastal city.

Karla stopped to admire the blazing scarlet hibiscus blooms and to pinch some dying leaves from the plant. She loved the richness of the lush tropical vegetation. *I don't need a green thumb to grow things here*, she mused. A shouting voice jolted Karla from her quiet enjoyment. An excited Seigi, standing at the edge of the small clearing that surrounded their home, was beckoning to them. Seigi's eyes radiated a wild, sad terror.

"Come, come!" he shouted, frantically waving them toward the house and toward the small room they used for translation work. Hank had built their breezy mountain bungalow from wood harvested from the surrounding trees. With its thatched roof and hard dirt floors, their home was the quintessential missionary dwelling. Hank enjoyed showing slides of it during furloughs in the States. An integral part of the home was the translation room—the "brains of the bungalow" Hank called it. Sergei hurried them to the door.

They rushed into the translation room. The shelves, the tops of three desks, and parts of the floor were cluttered with translation guides, Bible commentaries, various translations of the Bible, pages of discarded papers and notebooks. Sergei was pointing toward many worn notebooks that lined one shelf with uncharacteristic neatness. These notebooks were filled with the world's only written translation in the Vahudati language of the Gospel of John. Seigi picked a notebook up and fanned its pages as Hank and Karla looked on. Every page was blank. Seigi was crying as he picked up another, then another. All of the notebooks were empty.

Hank looked both confused and angry. Karla sank to her knees, head in her hands, joining Seigi with her quiet, bewildered crying. All their translation work was gone.

"Who did this?!" Hank blurted out, seeing but hardly believing his eyes.

Seigi handed Hank two well-worn English New Testaments they used in translation work. In both Bibles the pages where John's

Gospel should be were totally blank except for verse numbers and cross-references.

Hank stepped to their shortwave radio and called the missions compound in Nabire.

"We have a serious problem up here," he stammered into the microphone, "Let me speak to Raymond." Raymond Short was the field director for all Bible translation work in their region of Irian Jaya.

"Raymond, this is Hank. We've got a problem up here. All our work on the Vahudati language is gone! Seigi discovered it first and just showed us. All our work on the Gospel of John is gone."

"Hank, hold on, man. I understand. We've got something crazy going on down here, too. All of our Bibles are blank where John's Gospel should be. I've never seen anything like this. No one can find a word of John's Gospel in any of our English Bibles or tribal translations. This is simply crazy!"

"Ray, what is this? What's happening?"

Hank placed the microphone in its cradle on the radio. He slowly sank to the floor. His mind raced through the years of the often tedious and sometimes thrilling translation work. Each translation breakthrough had been glorious, fulfilling and rewarding. Now each empty page was a piece torn from his heart. He looked over at Karla who sat stunned, her eyes watery and red from crying. Hank was so paralyzed by the shock of the loss of their work that he had no energy to move and comfort her.

○ ○ ○

Dr. Harold Alexander Johnson, both brilliant and demanding, exuded a mysterious magnetic attraction that drew trembling seminarians who dared to take the risk of signing up for his Greek classes. Rumor among the students was that Dr. Johnson wasn't just a teacher; he was a flying leap off a high cliff. His classes were assignments in biblical wonder and academic trauma.

And today. After a few weeks of reviewing key features in Greek grammar, today was the day when he started his renowned exegesis in the Gospel of John class. Wary students, wandering in, proudly toting their first Greek New Testaments, and finding their seats, knew through the grapevine the challenge before them. They would have to do their own translation of the text from the Greek into English, being able to explain in class the grammatical, lexical, and exegetical contribution of each term in the Gospel. All this had to be done with awareness, also, of the historical and cultural issues attendant to the text. Yet, as imposing as these demands were, students who survived the class came away breathlessly in love with Jesus Christ, with a deep respect for the Word of God, and with a profound admiration for Dr. Johnson, whose teaching style literally provoked students to break out sweating in class. His brilliant mind and Socratic method, his grasp of the Greek language and first century biblical culture, and his passionate devotion to Jesus created traumatic amazement in his students.

Dr. Johnson said, "Open your Greek text to John 1:1."

Resistant to new fangled teaching tools like overhead projectors and, God forbid, computerized PowerPoint presentations, Dr. Johnson turned to write a word on the blackboard with chalk. (He also did not like whiteboards with felt-tipped markers.) He wrote the opening words of John 1:1: $\varepsilon v \ \alpha \rho \chi \eta \ \eta v \ o \ \lambda o \gamma o \sigma$. "In the beginning was the word . . . ."

Something astounding happened as he wrote. By the time he wrote the words $o \ \lambda o \gamma o \sigma$, the words $\varepsilon v \ \alpha \rho \chi \eta \ \eta v$ disappeared in order, word after word. Dr. Johnson wrote the same Greek words again on the board and in the same way they faded completely from sight.

Gazing at his hand and then turning to the students with a look of confused irritation, he snapped the chalk in two and blurted out, "Who put this disappearing chalk up here? I don't have time for these fun and games!"

Silence.

Disappearing chalk?

In a tentative, shaky voice a student said, "Sir, I've turned to John 1:1 in my Greek text and there are no words on the pages; just some letters and numbers at the bottom of the page."

The student was looking at the Greek text apparatus. Ancient Greek manuscripts of Bible books were handwritten by scribes. Inevitably human error or intentional changes crept into the transmission history of the biblical texts as scribes through the centuries made copies of copies of copies. The apparatus informed the student of these various "readings" by a complex textual critical code of letters and numbers. Most new students would initially be confused by it.

Johnson scowled and grunted. "If you had paid attention the past few weeks, you'd know that those 'letters and numbers' are called the apparatus, presenting the variants in the textual transmission of the manuscripts. What do you mean there are *no words* on the pages?"

Dr. Johnson picked up his own Greek text and opened to John 1:1. He then quickly scanned through the rest of John's Gospel. He stopped and looked down at his desk and then up at the ceiling and finally out at his stunned students who by this time had all thoroughly checked their own Greek New Testaments. No one had the text of John's Gospel before them. Empty pages all.

Silence.

"Well, I, I don't know what to say," Dr. Johnson quietly said with a strange sadness in his voice. "I—"

At that moment a colleague unexpectedly pushed open the classroom door.

"Harry, would you come with me, please? Something very strange is going on in Wyatt's "Survey of the Gospel of John" class. Students are reporting blank pages in their Bibles where John's Gospel should be."

○ ○ ○

"Jesus loves the little children, all the children of the world. Red and yellow, black and white, they are precious in his sight, Jesus loves the little children of—the— wo-r-r-l-l-d-d!"

"Very good singing, children," Nancy DeLano clapped softly, as a big, bright smile spread across her face. "You may be seated and we'll learn today's Bible verse."

When the six children settled into their places before her on the living room floor, Mrs. DeLano smiled down at them thinking, *They look like the little wooden letters on the tray when I play Scrabble.* Timmy, with his blond hair and blue eyes and wiggly energy, was a "second year" attender; Brent, Timmy's little buddy, was new this year and liked to be the entertainer, making the girls laugh. Brent had red hair and freckles and a never-fading smile. Sylvia and her sister, Lily, were returning twins, wearing pigtails with white bows and matching blue shorts and white tops. Sylvia was shy, but Lily was the just the opposite—she could make friends with a rock. Gita was a new girl to the club. She had deep black hair and rich, large brown eyes. Her family moved into the neighborhood five months earlier. They had moved from Madras, India. Next to Gita sat another new girl, Shannon, who lived in the apartments with her mother. Her parents had recently divorced and there was a soft sadness in Shannon's eyes. *I hope I can be an encouragement to her and to her mother,* Nancy prayed.

Nancy again gently clapped her hands and announced that they would memorize John 3:16.

"Boys and girls, this verse is one of the most famous verses in the Bible. It tells us of God's great love for the world and for each one of you. I'll put the words on the board and we can learn it together."

Nancy turned toward the three-legged easel where she had placed her white board, and began sticking large magnetic word cards to the smooth surface. *FOR—GOD—SO—LOVED—THE—WORLD—* As she did so, she smiled to herself. She loved children; she loved teaching them about God and his wonderful plan of salvation. For twelve years now, she had been holding Child Evangelism Bible clubs in her home. Lincoln Elementary, the local public school, released the children thirty minutes early each Thursday so they could attend the Bible club. Yet after all this time, she was still deeply thrilled each time a child understood how much God loved him or her. She marveled at their innocent faith and their receptivity to God. *THAT—HE—GAVE—HIS—ONE—AND—ONLY—SON—*

When all the words were on the board, Nancy led the children in reciting the verse.

"Now, let's read it one more time and then I'll turn all the cards over and we'll begin to memorize it." The children said the verse in sweet, raggedy unison.

When all the cards were turned over so that only the blank backsides were showing, she asked the children what the first word was. "Raise your hand to answer," she reminded.

"For!" blurted out a freckled-faced boy with a tousle of red hair.

"That's right, Brent, but please raise your hand so I can call on you."

Brent's face flushed with shame, as a few kids teased the normally "Mr. Perfect" for his little mistake.

"Okay, yes. The first word of our verse is 'for'." In one fluid motion she took the magnetic card down, flipped it over, and re-stuck it on the board. She raised her voice to be heard over the teasing and to draw everyone's attention back to the verse. "Now, what is the next—"

She did a double-take, and cast a puzzled glance at the board. That first card was still facing blankside-out. She snatched the card from the board and turned it over and over again. The card was blank on both sides. She definitely had everyone's attention now. There was a moment of quiet wonder, and then—

"Mrs. DeLano, are you doing a magic trick?"

"Cool!"

"Do it again!"

"Yay! Magic!"

Nancy laughed off their barrage of questions—and tried to laugh off the nervous confusion sneaking up her spine. "No, no, kids, I'm not doing magic. I, uh, I—well, now, does anybody remember the second word of our verse?"

A hand shot up.

"Yes, Silvia, what is it?"

"God?" Silvia offered shyly.

Picking up the magnetized card, Nancy flipped it over slowly and looked at it wide-eyed before she stuck it back on the board.

"Yay! You did it again, Mrs. DeLano."

"It *is* a trick!"

"Where did you learn magic, Mrs. DeLano?"

"Can you make *me* disappear?"

"How do you do it? Show us how!"

"Yeah, show us! Show us!"

The din of the children's excitement faded as her pounding heart throbbed loudly in her ears. What is going on? Reaching out a trembling hand, she quickly turned over the remaining cards. Much to the delighted surprise of the children—who gave her performance a thunderous standing ovation—all of them were blank on both sides. She took a few steps backward and slumped down quietly into a rocking chair.

"Are you okay, Mrs. DeLano?" dear little Timmy asked, nudging the others and shushing their excited frenzy. "Sh-h-h, you guys, something's wrong. What is it, Mrs. DeLano?"

Nancy sighed and lifted up her bowed head, forcing herself to give a reassuring smile to her little class. "Why don't we have our cookies and juice now, children?" In the kitchen, after serving up the snack, Nancy went to the phone and called her husband.

"Jim, you're not going to believe this . . ."

○ ○ ○

SEPTEMBER 26
"This is an utter outrage!" shouted Cardinal Joseph Santini. He stood at the head of a huge polished mahogany table, set in the center of a solemn and scholarly conference room—deep crimson wallpaper, heavily-draped windows, gold lamp fixtures. The room's atmosphere, normally as calm as the Galilee Sea after Jesus stilled the storm, crackled with electric tension as he glared into the pallid faces of the fourteen dedicated scholars seated around the table. Rarely were all the members of the Vatican's Pontifical Biblical Commission summoned at the same time. They had been hastily gathered to consider a very troubling situation.

Cardinal Santini continued in red-faced bluster. "We can't just have biblical texts disappearing all over the world!"

"We are getting reports from every continent that the Gospel of John has simply vanished," added Cardinal Lesewicz. He continued, "We have checked both ancient manuscripts and codices as well as various translations in Latin, Greek, Spanish, and English and we

Cardinal Rodenzinger, an old, quiet, and thoughtful man known for exceptional diligence in biblical and theological insight, locked eyes with McKinny. Rodenzinger had seen a lot over the years and was no stranger to controversy. Immovable as a Michelangelo statue, he stared back at McKinny and spoke with surprising calm.

"Never in the history of the Church has anything like this ever occurred. What is going on? Who knows? Who's to explain this? We are as ignorant as everyone else. We ourselves are only beginning to learn of this massive disappearance of a much-beloved Gospel. Maybe those in the Church who engage in study related to supernatural disturbances can offer some ideas."

"You mean those concerned with *Satan* and *demons*? You think this is demonic activity?" Cardinal Santini exclaimed.

Quietly, yet firmly, Rodenzinger answered, "It's a thought."

Cardinal Santini sat down, trying to grasp the magnitude of the issue before the Commission. *The Holy Father needs us now more than ever.* They had been quickly summoned to craft a paper that would help the Pope address a very jittery Catholic world. He worried, *What would the Holy Father say?*

● ● ●

"Good evening. This is Carl Wilson with *ABC World News Tonight*. We begin this evening with an unusual and alarming religious story. World leaders of various segments of the Christian faith are staggering under the unexplainable worldwide disappearance of one of the four Gospels from the Bible—apparently the Gospel of John has totally evaporated. Vatican scholars are feverishly endeavoring to prepare the Pope to address the world. Asked about this strange phenomenon, the Reverend Jimmy Blake, son of world-renown evangelist Truman Blake, says it is too soon to offer any meaningful explanation as to why a portion of the Bible has vanished."

Ben Cook took another handful

"I don't know what Steve will say," Anne shrugged. "I wonder if anybody at all has an answer. Will all the biblical scholars in the world be able to explain this? I'd hate to be the Pope right now, or any Christian leader who has to seriously address this. It's frightening."

She took a bite of popcorn and a sip of Diet Coke. A curious, almost comical expression, spread across her face, as she tried to lighten the mood. "One thing you can bet on: this is going to bring out the kooks. And I can guess what's going to be all over the tabloids in the grocery store checkout lane."

Ben smiled wryly. "Oh, I can just imagine the headlines: 'Aliens Abduct the Bible.' It should make for some funny reading." His smile turned to a sober frown. "I'm sorry, honey, I just can't find it in me to laugh. This is horrible."

Back on the TV Carl Wilson paused mid-report to listen in his hidden earpiece. He looked startled as he turned to speak into the camera, "This just in. Reports are now coming into the Vatican that the book of Psalms is also disappearing from the Bible. We'll try to confirm these new reports as this unusual story continues to unfold.

"In other news, the president arrived in San Diego . . ."

Ben reached for his Bible. Muttering, "Esther, Job, Psalms . . ." he found the place and stared down at the pages. The report was right. The pages were blank. Every Psalm, all one hundred and fifty of them had disappeared from his Bible, leaving only the chapter and verse numbers, and the book name at the top of each page as evidence of what had once been there. Anne, looking on in wide-eyed shock, began to cry.

"What's happening, Ben? First the Gospel of John and now the Psalms. Our Bibles are disappearing! O God, what is going on?"

● ● ●

OCTOBER 3

For an October day in Jackson, Mississippi, it was unusually warm and humid, yet the uncomfortable heat couldn't deter a crowd of determined people from gathering at the Mississippi State Courthouse.

"Get the camera over here! Shoot it from this angle," yelled Tony Bohler, TV reporter for Channel 6 News in Jackson. Seeing the mass of praying bodies of Christians laying on the sidewalk and steps of the courthouse, Tony had mixed feelings about yelling across them to Jake, his cameraman. It seemed sacrilegious to Tony. He didn't want to inadvertently do something blasphemous. Governor Oliver Cavenaugh Wright had commissioned and set up a marble monument containing the Ten Commandments in the lobby of the courthouse. A legal battle ensued around the tenuous principle of the separation of church and state. Wright argued that he was merely honoring the high place that God and Scripture hold in the history of the American judicial system. The Mississippi Supreme Court had unanimously ruled against the monument, asserting that Governor Wright had overstepped his legal authority.

Throughout the proceedings, crowds had assembled here outside the courthouse daily, some offering prayers for and others shouting protests against the Ten Commandments monument. Rumor had it that some federal agents were coming today to take the monument out of the courthouse lobby. Christians had come from around the state to call upon God to preserve the right to have the Word of God publicly displayed. Some loyal intercessors had even come from other states, some as far away as Colorado. Tony wanted to get some good footage for the evening news. This was a hot story locally, for sure, and it was beginning to get national attention as well.

Getting into position, Jake started filming as Tony did a voiceover. "Hundreds of people have gathered once again here at the courthouse on this sunny Mississippi day to either pray for or stand against Governor Wright's controversial monument. For Wright and many Christians, the monument is a symbol of the American freedom to honor God and the Ten Commandments in our judicial system. Others strongly contend that Wright is violating the constitutional principle of the separation of church and state—a principle many Christians claim has been misinterpreted to actually violate the intention of this nation's Founding Fathers."

As Tony spoke, Jake scanned the crowd with his camera. Most were prostrate on the sidewalk or kneeling on the courthouse steps. Jake zoomed in on a middle-aged man with graying hair, dressed in a business suit, forehead on the pavement, face twisted in agony as he prayed to God.

"Hey, look at that!" someone shouted, pointing to the glass door entrance to the courthouse. As Tony and Jake turned toward the entrance, a tangle of shouting protesters surged toward Governor Wright as he came to the top of the steps.

"Separation of Church and State! Separation of Church and State!" they yelled as Governor Wright lifted his hands to quiet the crowd. The governor was surrounded by several armed guards and federal agents. Governor Wright began to speak.

"Get him, Jake. Get this on camera," Tony insisted.

"Ladies and gentlemen, listen to me, please," the governor spoke loudly, trying to be heard over the relentless clamor of protestors and supporters. "Something very strange has just happened. Several federal agents arrived and began to physically remove the monument. As they were detaching the monument from its foundation, the words engraved in the marble simply disappeared."

A noisy, collective gasp went up from the crowd, protesters and prayers alike.

"The words vanished as if . . . as if they had never been carved into the stone. I was shocked, as were the agents who saw this unusual thing happen right before their eyes."

Tony turned to Jake. Both had the look of winning a $100 million lottery.

"We have just made the 'big time'! This story has just gone to a whole new level, Jake. And we—hot dang!—we are here to report it!"

They began to quickly interview those in the crowd on both sides of the issue. After jotting down comments from four or five people, they huddled up and Tony quickly made a few notes for himself.

"Okay. Let's do it, Jake!" Tony said excitedly.

Jake raised the camera, and cued Tony to begin. "The heated cultural controversy about the Ten Commandments being displayed in the Mississippi State Courthouse has strangely become a moot point. The words of the Ten Commandments, according to eyewitnesses, have simply disappeared from the controversial monument. No explanations have been given as to how this happened."

Tony glanced quickly down at his notes and then back up, looking directly into the camera lens.

"Advocates for posting verses of the Bible in this segment of the public square say they no longer have a reason or resource for their cause. Those protesting the monument, on the other hand, while admitting to being shaken by this unusual occurrence, believe this is a strange victory for their side."

● ● ●

OCTOBER 17

Wayne Unger and Luci Dykstra woke up groggily from another fitful night together to face another boring day. The two had met at My Baby's Blues, a popular Grand Rivers nightclub. Over a couple of drinks and friendly conversation about favorite songs, rock bands, life, and even religion, something had "clicked" for Wayne and Luci. After three more dates, Luci had moved into Wayne's old, but roomy, apartment located near the Grand Rivers Community College. That was six months ago.

Wayne had grown up Catholic and jettisoned his faith after high school—just like his older brother and sister had done. Wayne had never connected with the religious life and in recent years was particularly appalled by the sexual abuse scandals and hypocrisy of rogue priests. Religion—who needed it? He was enrolled in a few business courses at the community college and drove a delivery truck for a building products company. He didn't make a lot of money, but enough to pay rent, bills, and tuition and still have a little spending money. Now with Luci living with him and sharing the rent, life was good in some ways. But in other ways, life was far too routine and boring. Wayne felt the boredom soak in as he stretched to get up and get ready for work, and then fell back into the sheets.

Luci had told Wayne that she had grown up in a rigid Christian Reformed Church family. She remembered a persistently angry, but well-providing, father and a religiously devoted, but obsessively-controlling, mother. She said that her parents were well meaning, but nonetheless the home atmosphere made Luci and her sisters yearn to be on their own as soon as they could. At eighteen, she had moved out and lived here and there with some girlfriends from high school. She had dumped her religion because it had offered no love or meaning to her, but she still carried a low-grade guilt for doing so. For all the rules she rebelled against, Luci was still haunted by the reality of the God who loved her. She just didn't pay much attention to that reality anymore. She, too, worked sporadically on some college courses while earning money as a clerk at Pam's, an upscale clothing shop in Center City Mall. Now after four years of crash-and-burn relationships with guys, she found herself living with Wayne, wondering if this would be the man she would spend the rest of her life with. She stretched and got up to get some orange juice. While she too felt the hum-drum of another day, Luci wasn't so much bored as she was intensely uneasy about where her life was headed. The daily routine was a way for her to avoid thinking about her future.

"Turn on the TV, Luc'," Wayne said, "see what's on the news."

"Iraq is on the news, Wayne. Iraq, Iraq, Iraq," she said as she snapped on the TV.

On the screen, a local reporter standing near a large urban church was saying, ". . . totally disappeared. Religious experts—Protestant, Catholic, Orthodox, and Jewish—cannot explain why all the books of the Bible have vanished. While acknowledging the alarm this strange event has caused, many church and synagogue leaders, as well as other key people in the religious community, are urging people not to panic. Church leaders worldwide, I'm told, are meeting to discuss how to address this unparalleled situation. As Erik Swanson, pastor of the church behind me, said, 'It is a serious and severe challenge to face a world with no Bible.' Back to you, Susan."

Luci sat down on the edge of the bed, stunned by what she heard. "A world with no Bible," she muttered to herself, her mind reeling from the thought.

"What's wrong, Luc'?" Wayne asked.

"I can't believe this, Wayne. Did you hear what that reporter said? How can there be a world with no Bible?"

Wayne smirked and said, "Come on, Luc', what do you care if it's gone? It's not like we're reading it anyway. Let the religious people worry about it. Maybe the world will be a better place without it. Think of all the wars and bloodshed done in the name of God and religion."

"Yeah, I know, but still . . . no Bible. How could this happen?"

For Luci the world without a Bible felt somehow threatening and dark, like, if there was no Bible, then there was no God. She felt chilled inside, first feeling and then losing that haunting sense of the God who loved her. Was God gone?

Wayne saw the fear on her face.

"Luci, it happened. Don't worry about it. So the Bible is gone? Come on, we've had talks about religion. Where did it get us, huh? I was Catholic, you were Protestant, and we both felt like religion screwed us up."

"How can you say, 'Don't worry'? That guy just told us the Bible has vanished. No Bible. Doesn't that bother you?"

"No, it doesn't," Wayne said flatly, and he got up and started getting ready for work.

Luci sat on the edge of the bed, wondering if God had vanished, trembling inside. She felt sick and disoriented, free-floating like a tiny speck of a human being abandoned in a vast, obscure, and empty space.

"A world with no Bible," she quietly repeated as a tear slid down her cheek and puddled at the corner of her mouth.

2

UNEXPLAINABLE

OCTOBER 20

There was a presence about Steve Roberts. Six foot and lean; blond hair parted in the middle and combed back; blue eyes that caught light and turned it to crystal; a pleasant, resonant voice; Steve attracted attention. This morning in his grey slacks, blue Oxford shirt, and deep blue sweater-vest, he looked casual, yet in charge. In charge, however, was the last thing he felt right now. As he walked across the platform to begin another Sunday service of Three Rivers Community Church, he felt alien, outside himself, as if walking in a dream. *How many times have I made this short walk?* he wondered. *Several weeks ago I had to come out here when the Gospel of John disappeared. That had everyone in an uproar. And while John's disappearance was odd, it seemed manageable. Then the Psalms vanished. Next, the Ten Commandments. With each Sunday I felt a sense of the growing fear in the people. I feel it now. And once again I am on this short path.*

The three-year-old TRCC sanctuary pleased the eye, with its soft white walls and ceiling catching the light of six large and very ornate crystal chandeliers. On this Sunday morning, Steve could feel the odd disjunction in his church, a pleasant place, yet filled with deeply troubled people. Steve noticed the louder-than-usual noise of numerous conversations among the people who were huddled in tight-knit groups. They were showing one another their Bibles, pointing at the blank pages and wondering aloud about what was going on. Steve noticed some people on the verge of tears, others appeared frightened and bewildered, while others were sitting quietly, eyes closed, waiting.

As Steve stopped at center stage, some folks quieted and sat down, others continued standing and talking. Steve stretched out his hands in the blessing and declared, "This is the day the Lord has made."

Almost all of the church responded, "We will rejoice and be glad in it."

"All of you, please be seated."

Steve paused until all were settled and he allowed the silence to linger. He scanned slowly over the unusually crowded sanctuary. Many new faces were scattered throughout the congregation, sitting in the burgundy-cushioned wooden pews. New faces of people pressed into church by the unusual events reported in the media. So many of the others Steve knew well. They were waiting on Steve, their pastor, a spokesman for God, to speak some order into the threatening chaos swirling around them. He felt a lump in his throat and butterflies in his gut. Steve silently prayed, *O Lord Jesus, the Word made flesh, give me words for these times. I don't know what's going on and people smarter than me are more than puzzled by what's happened to the Bible. I feel way out of my league on this one. Help me, God.* Then he spoke.

"We, ummm, we all are experiencing something so much . . . so much bigger than our ordinary lives and little church are used to. Like you, I have watched the news reports about whole sections of our Bibles disappearing . . . just ceasing to be, and then, I have looked into my own Bible to verify that the news reports were true. First it was John's Gospel; then the Psalms. After that the books of Moses, the Pentateuch—Genesis, Exodus, Leviticus, Numbers, and Deuteronomy; then Hebrews, Matthew, and Revelation vanished. Now we've lost everything except Esther and one chapter of Genesis. The question 'Why?' is what we all are asking. Why are our Bibles disappearing? Why are these two portions left? Who or what is causing this unsettling thing to happen to our Bibles?

"I must be frank with you. This all scares me. I am as confused, bewildered, and upset as you. I've asked the Lord to help me comfort you today, to help me speak some semblance of order into this catastrophe, to speak words of peace and hope in the face of this awful, this despairing reality—our disappearing Bibles. What can I say? I, too, am groping for reasons, for meaning, for some explanation, and I am not finding them.

"I talked with Dr. Harold Johnson over at the seminary the other day. He's a godly man whom many of you know—a man that I deeply respect. God used him years ago to help create in me a passion for the Bible. As we talked, he admitted that all this—99% of the Bible out of print—profoundly baffles him. Many godly scholars that he knows are simply stymied. These same questions of 'what?' and 'why?' and 'how?' as you know, are being discussed by the best Jewish, Catholic, Orthodox, and Protestant biblical scholars in emergency meetings in Los Angeles, Rome, and Jerusalem. If any answers can possibly be found to these confounding perplexities, surely they could find them. Still, from what Dr. Johnson said, there doesn't appear to be much hope of their coming up with anything. The Pope is baffled; leading evangelist, Truman Blake, simply weeps; Rabbi Ben Jakobi pleads ignorance.

"As I have asked God to help me know what to do today, I got an idea. Let me suggest we do something out of the ordinary since these are not ordinary days. Turn in your Bibles to where the Psalms should be. I know that you will find blank pages. Yet, there is a Psalm that is still there. It's Psalm 23.

"You don't see it, yet you know it. You sense its reality even now as we feel that we are globally in a shadowy darkness that smells of death. Let's declare what is true of our God, of our Lord Jesus Christ, the Great Shepherd. Let's stand and recite from memory Psalm 23."

The congregation stood. Many, looking down into their Bibles, still found it hard to believe that the words had really vanished. Yet the block of blank space after the "Psalm 23" heading spoke the unbelievable truth. Steve began the Psalm and together the congregation joined in. Their voices blended into an earnest and passionate assault upon the fears and turmoil that they all were feeling.

> *The LORD is my shepherd, I shall not be in want.*
> *He makes me lie down in green pastures,*
> > *he leads me beside quiet waters,*
> *he restores my soul . . .*

Many began to weep quietly as the words of the familiar Psalm filled the sanctuary.

> *He guides me in paths of righteousness*
> > *for his name's sake.*
> *Even though I walk*
> > *through the valley of the shadow of death,*
> > *I will fear no evil,*
> > *for you are with me . . .*

Steve could sense a growing strength and confidence in the people's voices.

> > *. . . your rod and your staff,*
> > *they comfort me.*
> *You prepare a table before me*
> > *in the presence of my enemies.*
> > *You anoint my head with oil;*
> > *my cup overflows.*

The passion in the voices of the congregation surged; they almost shouted the final words, speaking them out with joyful intensity and hope.

> *Surely goodness and love will follow me*
> > *all the days of my life,*
> > *and I will dwell in the house of the LORD*
> > *forever.*

"Brothers and sisters, hear me," Steve declared. "Psalm 23 can never vanish from the earth! It will never depart from this church and from our lives. Let me ask you: has anyone here memorized other Psalms?"

An awkward silence filled the room. Then a voice rang out.

"I know Psalm 139 by heart," declared Julia Olson.

"I know Psalm 51," Jeffrey Wells said in his deep, radio-announcer kind of voice.

"Psalm 42," Bill Randall said.

"Psalm 27," claimed Anne Cook. Ben turned and looked at her.

"Surprise," she whispered to him smiling.

Steve broke in, "See, folks, the written words may be gone, but we have the Word here," he said tapping his chest. "We will not, must not be afraid."

◦ ◦ ◦

The Reverend Randy Joe Jason, known by his followers as "Brother Randy Joe," had a cable TV program called *God's Warriors of Fire*, broadcast from a gaudy studio set made to look like a Victorian sitting room. With his flashy suits and immaculate hair resembling a puffy, smooth wad of yellow cotton candy, Brother Randy Joe of Oklahoma City was a Bible-pounding, sin-hating, Satan-fighting, glory-loving, Jesus-following, preaching machine. He was a boisterous and self-proclaimed "man of just one Book." He always closed his show by poking his open Bible toward the camera so that the Bible filled his viewers' TV screens. Then he made his thunderous affirmation in his southern drawl, "I jest *lo-o-ve* the *Bi-ible!*" Multitudes of people, by tuning in, demonstrated that they loved Brother Randy Joe's love of the Bible.

Now Brother Randy Joe found himself in a bind. The Book he so desperately needed to keep afloat financially had completely disappeared—well, except for two random portions, but that just complicated matters. For every three letters he got from his followers asking him why the Bible had disappeared, he got one asking why Genesis 34 and the book of Esther were still there. His followers were confused and scared.

His accountant had shown him the books. The book of numbers—finances—did not look good. The money, normally flooding in because he proclaimed proudly and passionately that he was a man of just one Book, was drying up like a sun-baked creek bed. A vanishing Bible was icy water on the flaming zeal of *God's Warriors of Fire.*

Brother Randy's mind frantically raced, trying to salvage hope (and money) for his ministry. He *had* to give his viewers a reason, a good reason from the Book about *why* the Book was disappearing. He had to keep his audience watching and their faithful donations coming in.

A new idea exploded in his mind. He, in fact, had a brand new fight— the greatest spiritual conflict of our times—the battle for the vanishing Book!

Brother Randy clapped his hands and rubbed them together close to his face. Something was forming in his mind. He had a far away look in his eyes and, then, just the hint of a smile took shape on his lips. He was ready. It was time!

Looking straight into the camera, and with his best expression of fierce warrior determination on his face, Brother Randy began to speak.

"Fellow warriors of God, I, like you, have a very h-e-e-avy heart. But the heaviness can't quench the fire! Our much bel-o-o-oved Book has been taken from us bit by bit, until now only a small toehold is left to us. This is a serious battle! The very war for the holy Word! I'm here to tell you that I'm deeply entrenched against this, this robbery of divine truth. I will fight! I will fight to the death to get the Bible back!

"Now, I know that the best scholars in the world are trying their hardest to explain what's happening to the precious Word of God. But, as you know, they are coming up empty. They have no explanations. None! Like clouds promising rain, they leave us dry, unsatisfied, sweating in this wasteland of Wordlessness." Brother Randy mentally congratulated himself for coming up with that phrase—a wasteland of Wordlessness. He liked it.

"But I, I have been seeking the Lord—the Lord of the fiery armies of the vast heavenlies. He has spoken to me about this horrible crisis we face: a demonic crisis without our precious Book, the Bible. I was in the Spirit, deep in prayer, and Jesus came to me. Jesus himself reminded me of a story he once told. It is the parable of the sower and the seed."

With a choke in his voice and a tear in his eye, Brother Randy Joe continued, "I can't ask you to turn to it in your Bibles for all the Gospels are now gone. But I believe you recall the story. Jesus said that the sower was sowing seed and that the seed was the Word of God. Jesus went on to say that a certain kind of soil was so hard that the birds of the air came and ate the seed off that hard soil."

Now Brother Randy began to get agitated. He began to raise his voice. He stared into the camera while sweat rolled down his face. He thumped his Bible.

"Jesus, our Captain, told me what's going on. He told me the answer as to why-y-y-y the Bible is disappearing. Jesus told me so that I could tell you. I love the Bible. That's why I think Jesus told me. Are you ready for *h-i-i-i-s* answer? Let me ask you again, are you ready for the answer from *Je-e-e-zuz* himself?

"The Lord Jesus told me that *it's the Devil himself* who is taking the Bible away! That's right! The Devil, our adversary, that low-down thief who comes only to steal is the one behind this outrageous disappearance of our precious Book! In the parable, Jesus himself identified those wicked birds that ate the seed. Jesus said the birds symbolize the Devil who snatches away the Word! Satan is the low-down, dust-eatin', diabolical culprit stealing the Book!"

Brother Randy was on a holy rant. He shouted, assuring his TV audience that they could trust him on this because he, Brother Randy Joe, was trusting Jesus himself on this.

"All those smart scholars—Jewish scholars, Catholic scholars, Protestant scholars—who are meeting in the powerful cities of the world can't figure out what's happening to the Bible. But I, Brother Randy Joe Jason, a lowly and simple preacher here in Oklahoma, have it on the authority of Jesus himself.

"I ask you to join me in prayer . . . a Satan-binding warfare prayer. We shall storm heaven's gates and we shall prevail in prayer. We're gonna defend what little ground we have left and not let the enemy steal Esther or our last little bit of Genesis away from us. Not only that, we're also gonna ask the Lord of the Armies of Hosts to make Satan give us back our Bibles. We shall win this battle for the Book! To do so, we need to keep on praying. And I ask you, I urge you to keep on giving so that we, you and me together, can win this fight. I need your financial help if this war is to be won soon. Send that check for $500 or $1,000. Some of you can send me $5,000 today. As Jesus said, 'Lay up for yourselves treasure in heaven.' Do it now, my fellow warriors. Write that check today so we can get the Bible back from the Devil's hands."

Hugging the Bible close to him, Brother Randy shouted, "I jest *lo-o-ve* the *Bi-ible!*" Then his red, sweaty face faded from view.

Ben Cook changed channels on his TV until he found a golf tournament.

"Well, Anne, you were right about this whole thing bringing the kooks out."Anne nodded her head. "Yeah. He sounds so sincere and passionate, like he really is trying to fight a real war for the Bible, but you know it's all entangled with his pitch for money. Still, what if he's actually right? What if the Devil is the one making the Bible disappear?"

"Honey, I don't know if he's right or not. Sounds an awful lot like a tabloid headline to me." Ben laughed, then fell quiet as he shrugged and shook his head. "Still, Jesus did tell that story about the Devil snatching away the Word. It *seems* like it applies to what's happening. I just don't know."

○ ○ ○

OCTOBER 22
Steve Roberts tossed and turned in his bed, unable to sleep, unable to stop his mind from spinning out of control. *What am I going to do? I've spent my life studying and teaching the Bible. Now it's gone. I can't handle my own fear much less the fear in the church.*

He turned his pillow looking for that cool spot to ease the heat he felt in his face. He kicked off the covers, feeling hemmed in by their presence.

"What's wrong, honey?" Betsy asked in a husky, sleep-filled voice.

"I can't stand this, Bets'. I don't know what I'm going to do. What's going to happen to our ministry? With no Bible to teach and preach, I'm headed for joblessness."

"That's not true, Steve, and you know it. People are looking to you now more than ever. They need you, sweetheart."

"That's just it. They need me. Need me for what? For answers! And I don't have any. I don't know what in the hell is going on. It scares me . . . a lot. What does this mean for our future? What am I going to do?"

"Steve, one day at a time. The people don't expect you to have answers. Tell me, who has answers for this . . . this . . . horrible situation? The best minds in the world are engaged in finding answers, and they haven't found any. No one in the church is going to hold anything against you. It's not your fault. Come on now, get some sleep."

"I can't sleep, Bets'. I just can't sleep."

Steve got out of bed, slid his feet into his slippers and wandered down the hall to his small home office. He sat at his desk in the dark. The moon cast a light blue banner of cool light across the room. Steve opened his Bible and slowly leafed through the pages. Page after empty page. The whiteness and emptiness of each page triggered and fueled a massive, rumbling, tumbling anxiety in him. *What am I going to do? This book is my life; my vocation; my calling. Now it's blank. God, what is going on? You said, "My word will never pass away." Is that a joke, God? Are you toying with us? Look, for all intents and purposes, it has passed away. It's not here, except for Esther and Genesis 34. What's up with that, God? The Bible is not here as it once was. What am I going to do?*

"Daddy, what's wrong?"

Steve, startled at the voice, turned to see Zachary, his five-year-old son, standing in the doorway.

"Oh, Zach, Daddy just can't sleep tonight. I thought I'd come down here for a while. I didn't want to keep Mommy awake."

"You look sad, Daddy. Are you okay?"

He walked over to Steve and climbed up into his lap. Steve embraced him and gazed out the window at the moonlit night.

"Zach, Daddy is not okay. I love the Bible and it's gone."

"I know, Daddy. My Bible has empty pages, too. But I still talk to Jesus. Is that okay?"

"Of course, that's okay, Zachy. Daddy is just thinking about his job. My job is . . . is to teach the Bible and to help people live by the Bible. I'm just wondering what my job will be now that there is just a tiny bit of the Bible left."

Zach scrunched up his face in confusion. "Daddy, do you *have* to have a Bible to be a good pastor?"

Steve was stopped both by the innocence and question of his son. *Do I have to have a Bible to be a good pastor?*

"Zachy, I'll have to think about that. Now, you scoot along and get back to bed. Be quiet and don't wake up Zoe. I love you."

"I love you too," Zach hugged his dad's neck, and walked sleepily out of the office. When he reached the doorway, he turned around. "Don't be sad, Daddy. I think you're a good pastor."

Alone in the office, Steve bent his head down on his folded arms, and resting on the desk, began to cry. *Oh, God, what am I going to do?*

The gripping, churning anxiety would not go away. His mind would not stop spinning. His stomach cramped. *I've got a family. God, this is all I've ever wanted to do. It's all I know how to do. I never, never imagined ministry without a Bible. Oh, God, help me to go on. Little Zach thinks I can be a good pastor even without the Bible. What do you think, heavenly Father? Will you help me? I feel like I am traveling in a new kind of wilderness. I am not going to stop, sit down and give up. I won't do it. I still have you, God, even if I don't have a Bible. You will have to be my only hope and sufficiency. I ask you to, please.*

Steve went to bed and fell asleep.

○ ○ ○

NOVEMBER 1

The executive offices of Somervell Publishing of Grand Rivers, Michigan, were in a state of pandemonium. Clint Kessler, the president, and his team of VPs, could not get their minds around what was happening. The lifeblood of their publishing enterprise had all but drained away.

The company's constant bestseller had been a modern version of the Bible in numerous editions—study Bibles for men, for women, for students, for pastors. From the first days when the Gospel of John began to vanish, Clint and other executives received reports of strange occurrences from their publishing sites. Whole pages of biblical text were unexplainably lost from the computers; massive printing press drums went blank; some Bibles were coming from production with whole sections of wordless pages and other editions had just the Bible study notes in the margins of the pages. The Word of God was gone, but the words of people offering insights and background information printed nicely.

Somervell was not alone. All other publishers of Bibles and biblical literature were scrambling to adjust to the cataclysmic loss of the Scriptures. Every version, every translation, every paraphrase, every written verse in any language known was gone. Every direct quote from the Bible whether in commentaries, Bible study reference books and CDs, daily devotionals, on Bible memorization cards, on Internet websites, and even hand-scribbled road signs was gone. Popular books by Philip Yancey, Max Lucado, Chuck Swindoll, Beth Moore, and so many other authors had gaping blank sections where the Scriptures had been quoted. With the mysterious exception of Esther and Genesis 34, the written Word of God no longer could be found on the earth. Any attempt to print or even handwrite it proved futile. The words would instantly disappear. The only medium it could still be found in was the human voice.

An employee rolled in a cart with bottles of water, cans of soda and two coffee urns, cups and sugar and cream. Clint got up and poured himself a cup of coffee—black—and looked at his beleaguered team. With strain and worry in his voice Clint said, "Ladies and gentlemen, it looks like we're going to have to shut down operations. Bible publishing is facing a crisis unheard of in history. I'm sorry. I don't know what else to do."

Clint slowly sat down and a heavy, almost suffocating silence enveloped the conference room.

● ● ●

Khallad Majdi Rakhshan, a renowned Islamic scholar and recognized spokesman for the Muslim religious world, sat across from Lawrence Kingsley. The program *Lawrence Kingsley Live* wanted to preempt the other networks by being the first to televise an official response from the Islamic faith about the disappearance of the Jewish and Christian Scriptures.

"You've heard the reports as we have, Mr. Rakhshan . . . or is it Reverend? So, what do you make of this unusual event?" Lawrence Kingsley asked his guest.

"You may just call me Khallad which means 'old' or 'revered,' Mr. Kingsley. And I admit that I do feel old in the face of such strange and troubling occurrences. First, let me say on behalf of all of the Muslim world that we are very saddened by the disappearance of the Bible—the Jewish Scriptures and the Christian New Testament. We Muslims deeply honor our holy word, the Koran, and we cannot imagine a world without it. We wish that this was not happening to the Jews and Christians."

"Yes, but do you and other Islamic scholars have any idea as to why this has happened or who did it? I understand that the best scholars of Christendom are at a loss as to the answers to these questions."

Khallad Majdi Rakhshan seemed to squirm as Lawrence Kingsley asked the question again. The Islamic scholar appeared like he didn't want to hear it, much less answer it.

Kingsley pressed in, "Well, do you? Do you have any thoughts as to why this is happening?"

Khallad took a deep breath and spoke, avoiding any direct look into the camera.

"Many of our best scholars and historians, while considering many things about this loss of the Bible, seem to gather around the same idea as to why it *may* have happened. I stress the word 'may' because they are not in total agreement about this."

"About what?" Kingsley asked.

"Well, our best scholars think that the disappearance of the Jewish and Christian writings is an act of Allah, the only blessed God. Allah, as an act of judgment against Christians and Jews for all the violence they have perpetrated against our peoples throughout many eras of history, including today in Gaza and around Jerusalem, has taken their Bibles away."

"What? The Bible has vanished as a judgment of Allah against Jews and Christians. Are you . . . your scholars serious about this?" Lawrence Kingsley seemed incredulous.

"Well, as I said, this is only a tentative reason that our scholars offer to the world. We know that it is quite abrasive, yet we can think of no other reason as compelling. Perhaps Jews and Christians will look more sympathetically at the Palestinian question. Also, it seems your country's needless invasion of Iraq has disturbed Allah as well. Allah is the sole God of justice. Perhaps Allah is remembering the crusades, too, when so many Arabs were violently killed."

Kingsley bored in. "Wait a minute. Are you saying that Muslims have never acted violently against Christians and Jews? I think to be fair you need to acknowledge Islamic violence as well. Elementary students of history know of violent acts against others in the name of Allah. You even have a term for it—*jihad*, or holy war."

"That is true, Mr. Kingsley, but here's the point: the Koran has not disappeared, but the Jewish and Christian holy writings, for all intents and purposes, have vanished. As I said, it seems that Allah, in strict justice, has acted."

Ben Cook punched the button on his remote and gulped his soda.

"That is ludicrous! I can't believe that guy! Allah has taken the Bible away from Christians and Jews? This is inflammatory! Outrageous! I can't believe he actually said what he said to a watching world."

"Calm down, Ben," Anne coaxed. "He is just speaking the 'party line' of the Muslim world right now. Why should we be surprised? The Muslims have a chance to score for their team and their god Allah. And they're doing it."

"Yeah, but what about 'we're very saddened by the disappearance of the Bible'? He doesn't sound very saddened to me. Like you say, he sounds triumphant. What a jerk!"

"Oh, come on, Ben, let it go. At least we now have two reasons why we have no Bible: the Devil and Allah."

Anne took their empty glasses and walked toward the kitchen.

"I can't believe that guy! 'Allah, in strict justice, has acted.' Sheer idiocy!"

"Let it go, Ben, just let it go," Anne called from the other room.

● ● ●

NOVEMBER 7
Steve Roberts leaned back on his sofa and looked around his living room. Dr. Johnson and his wife, Marty, were sitting on the loveseat across from him. Harold Johnson's teaching schedule at the seminary had been radically reduced in light of the disappearance of the Greek text of the New Testament. Many seminaries and Bible schools were in turmoil, trying to adjust curriculum schedules that required deleting the Bible-content intensive courses. Many teachers were without subjects to teach and school administrations faced letting teachers go. Thankfully Harold Johnson also taught two master's level courses in first-century Palestinian history and culture. Those classes still met.

Nancy DeLano and her husband, Jim, sat in chairs next to the Johnsons. The Johnsons and DeLanos were talking about the unusual event at the Jackson, Mississippi courthouse.

Ben and Anne Cook were beside Steve on the sofa. Steve's wife was in the kitchen making some coffee for the group. She could squeeze in later next to Steve on their large sofa. Next to the Cooks, in a chair near the sofa, sat Tracy Myers, daughter of missionaries Hank and Karla Myers. She was living with her aunt and uncle, the DeLanos, and attending a local Christian high school. She had recently received an e-mail from her parents that reported the loss of all their work in translating the Gospel of John for the Vahudati people. Tracy sat there in quiet turmoil. *Why God would allow such a devastating thing to happen to Mom and Dad, and to the Vahudati people?*

The group usually consisted of the Cooks, Johnsons and DeLanos and they met weekly to share what was going on in their lives and to pray together. Steve encouraged small groups to develop so that folks could learn to practice biblical community. He would often tell the church, "Face to face is transformational space" or "Small is big to

God." Steve's group would often discuss the Sunday message, or a current event, or any topic suggested by someone on the spot. The group wanted to share life together more than learn more stuff together. The disappearance of the Bible was the hot topic. Steve had invited Tracy to join them because he had heard of her parents' deep discouragement at the loss of their translation work.

"Okay, let's get started," Steve said.

"We, like so many others, face a dilemma as a church. So many people are perplexed, and riddled with fear and even anger. Ben, you and Anne were the first ones to contact me about this. And my phone has been ringing off the wall ever since then with people wanting answers. Answers I can't give. So, I've asked Dr. Johnson if he would be open to answering any questions that we have about this scary event. He tells me that he has been in almost constant conversation with other scholars and leaders about the Bible's disappearance. It seems that no one knows why the Bible, except for Esther and Genesis 34, has disappeared. "

"Brother Randy Joe Jason has an answer," Anne Cook was troubled. "You know, that guy on TV that "jest *lo-o-ves* the *Bi-ible*"? Well, he's convinced that the Devil has taken the Bible away. Ben and I have talked about it, and even though Brother Randy comes across as a wacky, money-grabbing televangelist, at least he's able to suggest a reason for all of this. And, well, it seems plausible. What do you think, Pastor Steve?"

Harold Johnson jumped in as Steve was about to speak.

"Before you answer that, Steve, let me offer a comment on it."

"Go right ahead, Dr. Johnson," Steve offered.

"I've been thinking a lot about this crisis. As you said, I've been meeting with many colleagues. Spontaneous gatherings are cropping up everywhere. So far, all I can say is that we are totally stymied by the Bible going out of print. "

Turning toward her, Dr. Johnson said, "Now, Anne, let's think the Reverend Jason's reason through. I have heard that he used Jesus' parable of the sower and the seed to come up with his, what you call, 'plausible' explanation. Reverend Jason asserts that the Devil has snatched the Word away from the world, just like the birds snatched away the seed from the path. That is the reason he gives for why the Bible has disappeared.

"Now, for argument's sake, let's imagine that is true. With all we know about Satan and his wicked ways and schemes, where would he ever get the *authority* and power to do such a drastic deed? This is an unparalleled catastrophic event—the disappearance of the written Word of God.

"Basic teachings of our theology affirm that while Satan acts against God, he can only do so as God allows that activity. You recall the opening story in the book of Job. We also know that God is deeply identified with his Word and Jesus himself taught the indestructibility of it—'heaven and earth will pass away, but the Word of God remains forever.' Forever, Anne. But now it's gone. And, according to Reverend Jason, Satan somehow did it? Has the Devil acted independently of our sovereign God and done something God himself said would never be done?"

Betsy came in with the coffee.

"Perfect timing, Bets'," Steve said with an uneasy smile. "We are in the throes of some heavy conversation—a talk that is just right for a strong, caffeine jolt." Everyone smiled with Steve, except Anne and Tracy.

"Are you saying, Dr. Johnson, that Satan isn't behind the disappearance of the Bible?" Anne pressed in with irritation in her voice. "At least Brother Randy—I can't believe I am defending him—is trying to answer the burning question of *why* the Bible's gone. That's what everybody wants to know. It's what I want to know."

Tracy spoke up, "My parents are in agony over losing all their work for the Vahudatis. Dad's dream to see this unreached people group come to know Jesus has turned to a nightmare. While he's confused about what happened, he too, cannot rule out that Satan somehow doesn't want the Vahudatis to become Christians. He believes something very sinister is behind the disappearance of all their translation work."

Dr. Johnson responded, "Anne, Tracy, let me be clear and honest here. All I can offer are some thoughts in the making. I am not trying to say Brother Randy is wrong. I just want us all to think these things through. I am not saying *for certain* that Satan isn't somehow in on this. What I am saying, however, is that if Satan is behind this, then some major theological fault-lines are shifting."

"What do you mean, Dr. Johnson, by fault-lines shifting?" Tracy asked.

Harold took a sip of coffee and continued.

"We have always been taught that Satan cannot act outside God's controlling will. In some mysterious way Satan accomplishes exactly and only what God wants Satan to accomplish. Like I said, remember the Book of Job? God told Satan that he could do so much and no more. If Satan has caused the Bible to disappear, something God said can never happen, then Satan somehow is acting independently of God. For many scholars this is just unthinkable. Actually, they conclude that it is impossible. That's what I mean by a huge shift in our theology if Satan is behind this. Again, believe me, I am not sure how any of this can be taking place. But it is. I am groping my way along like everyone else.

"Well, if Satan isn't behind the total annihilation of the Bible, then that leaves us logically with God as the one behind it, doesn't it, Dr. Johnson?" Steve asked.

Nancy DeLano gasped and Jim squirmed in his seat.

"That can't be," Nancy cried out. "God would never take his Word from us like this. What kind of God is it that would give it and then take it away? That seems so cruel. I am so confused. I keep thinking of all the little children who need to hear the Word of God. I had to . . . had to stop hosting the children's Bible club in my home."

Nancy lowered her head and began to cry quietly. Jim reached over and held her hand.

"Nancy, I'm *not* saying that God has taken his Word away from us," Harold said gently. "Let me repeat: all I'm saying is that *I'm not sure what the answer is right now*. As inconceivable as it may sound, I don't think either Satan or God is behind this. But, of course, I could be wrong. I just don't know."

"Then who?" asked Ben. "Do you think that Islamic guy who was on Lawrence Kingsley is right? That Allah has done it as a judgment on Christians and Jews?"

Harold smiled and said, "I'll admit that that is one of the most intriguing reasons that I've heard. The God of Islam is in some sort of competition with the Judeo-Christian God. Allah is now settling some sort of historical score. 'Checkmate! I've got your Bible.' It's a very interesting twist on the age-old, Israeli-Arab conflict, but it is more inflammatory than explanatory. But, to me it is the least likely reason if our theology is right, Ben."

"Then I ask again, who *has* done this?" Ben pleaded.

"Then I'll answer again: I just don't know." Dr. Johnson sipped at his coffee.

"Well, here's something else I'm wondering about," Tracy spoke up. "Look, here in my Bible is the book of Esther. And back here, Genesis 34. If the Word of God is gone, why are these words still here? I've been told that neither Esther nor Genesis 34 mention God's name. Is that why they're still here?"

Jim chimed in. "Yeah, I just don't get it. A Catholic friend told me that a book called the Wisdom of Solomon disappeared from his Bible. I have never even heard of the Wisdom of Solomon as a Bible book. I am so confused. Does the fact that it disappeared mean that it should have been in our Bibles? And if so, what does that say about the fact that Esther and Genesis 34 are still there?"

Dr. Johnson was visibly fatigued from fielding such a wide range of weighty questions. "I know the Bible is both a divine and human book. It didn't just 'drop out of the sky' from God. There was tremendous interplay between God and human beings in the writing, collecting, and transmitting of the Bible. Now, not only are we facing the loss of the Bible, but with these random texts staying and disappearing, the whole doctrine of canonicity—what books comprise the Bible—is being questioned. This is massive. I was with some other Bible scholars recently and this issue came up as well—why Esther is here and Genesis 34 and why Wisdom of Solomon disappeared. We just don't know."

There was a sad mood over the room. Steve, normally a hopeful person, wanted to inject something positive and joyful into this bleak situation.

"Agnosticism in my old Greek professor," he chuckled. "I never thought I'd hear him say 'I don't know.' But hey, if we don't have a reason for how all this happened, let's make the best of the situation. We can still enjoy and reflect on God's Word. Anne, didn't you say Sunday that you have memorized Psalm 27?"

Anne shook her head yes.

"Would you recite it for us?"

Anne blushed and cleared her throat. "I've been working on this for the past few days as it dawned on me what a treasure I have stored in my memory. Please be patient with me as I try to recite."

Ben gazed at Anne in wonder, knowing how shy she was about this kind of thing. Dr. Johnson stared straight out, apparently thinking, while his petite wife, Marty, sat motionless. Nancy and Jim gripped hands even tighter. Tracy sat with her head bowed and her hands folded in her lap. Betsy and Steve sat, both with expressions of encouragement on their faces for Anne.

Anne spoke softly, yet with inner strength in her voice:

The LORD is my light and my salvation—
whom shall I fear?
The LORD is the stronghold of my life—
of whom shall I be afraid?

A deep, heart-settling peace descended on those in Steve's living room as Anne recited Psalm 27. When she finished, Steve spontaneously began singing, "He is Lord. He is Lord. He is risen from the dead and He is Lord. Every knee shall bow; every tongue confess that Jesus Christ is Lord." As he did so the others joined in. Somehow even in the face of the trauma of the absent Bible, a sense that things were still well permeated Steve's soul. Nancy DeLano relaxed and slipped her hand under Jim's arm and leaned on his shoulder. Tracy sat quietly praying that her parents would experience the same peace she felt right then. Ben, Betsy and the Johnsons sat with their eyes closed and with a look of deep contentment on their faces.

3

UNSTOPPABLE

NOVEMBER 9

The auditorium of the Grand Rivers Theological Seminary was packed with Protestants of the various denominations, Catholics of several major orders, Greek Orthodox priests, and even some Jewish scholars—all engaged in animated discussions. A consortium of these scholars, including Harold Johnson, who had serendipitously met one another three weeks before, had convened and had sent out invitations for this landmark meeting to as many biblical scholars in the Midwest as they could muster. The crowded auditorium was witness to both their hard work and the feeling of deep crisis in the Christian and Jewish world over the loss of the written Scriptures— Old Testament and New Testament.

Dr. Harold Johnson scanned the wide auditorium filled with leaders who wanted some direction regarding the missing Bible. His eyes then moved to those on his left—the members of the Committee. He recalled how he and these members of the Committee had been part of a hastily organized gathering of scholars at a large convention center in Chicago three weeks ago. This very group just happened to be at the same round table. Strangers to one another, yet not shy nor hesitant, they dove right into the topic at hand: what was going on with the Bible? Katherine Westbrook had spoken first.

"We have received some curious reports at our school," she said. "I'm Katherine Westbrook. I teach at East Lutheran Seminary in Toledo, Ohio." She was looking at Harold Johnson.

Harold responded, "I'm Harold Johnson. I teach at the Grand Rivers seminary in Michigan. What kind of 'curious reports' are you hearing, Dr. Westbrook?"

"You may call me Katherine. Well, it seems that the book of Esther has not disappeared. Television news reports are not exactly accurate. Reporters are saying that the entire Bible is gone, but the book of Esther is still present. All of it. A lot of people are asking why. Esther is a Bible book. Why is it still here? And another curious note is that the Wisdom of Solomon, a book that we Protestants hold to as one of the books of the Apocrypha *has* disappeared. The Apocrypha, twelve extra books in the Catholic Bible, is not considered authentic Scripture by Protestants even though English Bibles used to include them as a separate, non-inspired set of important religious writings. What are we to make of these oddities?"

Apparently Katherine's report was news to some at the table. Confusion marked several faces. The book of Esther, it was true, was considered a canonical book, that is, it was considered part of the God-inspired books. Yet it was *still* in print? The Wisdom of Solomon, a book that Jesus himself alluded to in the Gospels and that was declared to be Scripture by the Roman Catholic Church at the Council of Trent in the middle 1500s, disappeared, yet Wisdom of Solomon had never been endorsed as canonical by Protestants.

Another person spoke. "My name is Jakob Spielman of Temple Immanuel located in suburban Battle Creek, Michigan. I am a Rabbi and was once a professor of theology. Isn't the name of God totally absent from the book of Esther? I remember reading about some controversy about Esther, a debate whether it should be included in the Hebrew canon of Scripture."

Father James Pulaski had been a teacher and scholar of church history before taking leadership of the Grand Rivers diocese. He, too, was at the table. "It looks like Michigan is well represented at this table," he said with a grin. "I am Jim Pulaski, a Catholic priest. As I recall, the Council of Jamnia was convened by Jewish leaders after the fall of Jerusalem in AD 70. While there is some debate as to the extent that the Old Testament canon was established at the Council of Jamnia in AD 90, we know that Esther was hotly debated at that Council. Some questioned its canonicity, Rabbi Spielman, for the very reason you cited: there is no mention of the name of God in the book. The Song of Songs was questioned, too, at Jamnia because of its explicitly erotic content.

Jim Pulaski continued, "Yet, what is more puzzling to me about Katherine's 'oddities' is the fact that the Wisdom of Solomon has disappeared. If only canonical books—God's inspired Word—disappeared, why did only Wisdom of Solomon disappear? We Catholics consider all twelve of those books to be Scripture, but Protestants don't. Apparently we Catholics have not done our homework when it comes to canonicity. This is truly unbelievable."

Katherine Westbrook spoke again. "Friends, there's more. Here's another little oddity. Genesis 34 does not mention God's name either. It also tells about the ugly violence done by Judah and Simeon. Chapter 34 has not disappeared with the rest of Genesis. What are we to make of this anomaly?"

The final member at the table spoke up. "My name is Demitri. Demitri Kassius. I am with the Greek Orthodox Church in Lansing, Michigan. Katherine, I've heard that the Genesis 34 text may not have disappeared because of the ugly inhumanity recorded in it. It's not just that God's name is missing, it's the sickening violence so unworthy of God that is recorded there. Some think that chapter of the Bible could never have been inspired by God or even endorsed by God."

"Wait a minute! You're telling us that all of the book of Genesis disappeared except for one chapter? Chapter 34?" Harold Johnson asked in a surprised, but wearied voice.

"That is correct. That's the report we're getting from the field."

The group of scholars fell silent around the table. They were new friends who were facing a massive challenge.

A side door slammed somewhere off stage and the sound snapped Harold Johnson back into the present moment. The auditorium fell silent at the unexpected bang! of the door.

As Harold looked out upon the crowd, he knew that a lot of tension was coiled in the lives of those present; a tension sparked by the mysterious disappearance of the Bible and the ensuing fear of many, many people. Yet, Harold knew as well that many carried a ready eagerness to work together—as he and the Committee of Concern demonstrated—to thoughtfully address the crisis that permeated churches and academia, businesses and homes, and even individual hearts. Dr. Harold Johnson stood and approached the podium and tapped the microphone. "Ladies and gentlemen, please be seated."

A sudden burst of conversation erupted in the auditorium as people announced to one another that the meeting was convening. Just as quickly the auditorium got very quiet again. All eyes were fixed on Dr. Johnson.

"Ladies and gentlemen, aah umm, I mean, brothers and sisters, esteemed colleagues in the field of biblical studies—on behalf of the consortium who summoned you, I welcome you to this gathering of concerned scholars and spiritual leaders. On behalf of those with me on the platform, I say 'Thank you.' We are all here because we face a common and dreadful dilemma—the disappearance of the written Word of God. Yet, even more, we are here to encourage each other as we seek to address this dilemma and bring hope to those who are believers in God and who honor the Bible. Our diligent work together can help stem the fear, even panic, in many who profess the Jewish and Christian faiths in their varied expressions.

"We've named the assembled consortium the 'Committee of Concern' and they are seated behind me. We met just some weeks ago in Chicago. I am honored to introduce the Committee and, as I do, would the members please stand? Rabbi Jakob Spielman of Temple Immanuel near Battle Creek, Michigan; Father James Pulaski of the greater Grand Rivers diocese; Father Demitri Kassius of the Greek Orthodox Church of Lansing, Michigan; Dr. Katherine Westbrook, professor of biblical studies and oral traditions at East Lutheran seminary in Toledo, Ohio; and myself, Harold Johnson, professor of Greek and New Testament cultural studies here at this seminary.

"As you've perhaps noticed, we have Jewish, Protestant, Catholic, and Orthodox scholars here today. Setting aside our various and respected differences, we have anticipated, and yes, prayed, that you all will join in a unified effort to address this worldwide crisis of the written Word. Our pastors, priests, and rabbis—along with their alarmed congregations—are scrambling to make sense of this most unusual and unparalleled event. Never in the history of Judaism or Christendom has something like this occurred. It is incumbent upon us to face this unsettling situation and do so in such a way as to honor our God and to serve God's troubled people.

"At this time I want to invite Dr. Katherine Westbrook, professor of biblical studies and oral traditions, in Toledo, to come and address us. She will offer some direction for us to take. Dr. Westbrook."

Harold took his seat as his colleague approached the podium. Standing a moment in silence, Dr. Katherine Westbrook presented a commanding presence. She was tall with silver, swept-back hair and piercing blue eyes. She was dressed in a royal blue suit with a white blouse and a silver necklace and bracelet. Still stunning in her late forties, one could easily forget that she was a renowned biblical scholar and not a ladies' fashion magazine model.

"Esteemed colleagues, I am honored both by your presence here and by the opportunity to address you. What help, counsel, reason, and encouragement shall we offer to those reeling from the trauma of our lost Scriptures? I know that many are asking the ageless question: 'Why?' And, like you, I wish I could answer that question. But we cannot. So, in view of an almost completely vanished Bible, what do we do now?"

"As Dr. Johnson mentioned, I am a student of and professor in oral traditions. As you're all aware, no attempt to put the Word of God in writing is possible. In fact, all attempts to record the Bible in any way are futile. Many people in gatherings like this across our nation, yes, even across the world, have discovered that the only way to communicate the Bible is orally.

"Yet this is vital to remember: verbal communication of the Word is *not new*. All of our holy writings were preceded by a rich and varied oral tradition. The people of faith told stories from generation to generation, and at some point the stories were codified, that is, they were written down on whatever materials were available: clay tablets, parchment, papyrus, copper sheets. Most of the Bible was heard orally long before it was read. Much of the Bible's literary arrangement and poetic structure facilitated memory and oral transmission. As you know, very clear examples of this are the acrostic poems in the Scriptures.

"At various points in the transmission of God's Word, scribes began to put the stories and songs and prayers and genealogies into writing. Diligent scribes, knowing that they were transmitting the very words of God, faithfully, meticulously, even obsessively copied God's revelation letter by letter, word by word, story by story.

"Unexpectedly we find ourselves without the written Scriptures, and we find ourselves once again relying on oral communication. Yet please remember—this is not new. Many of us have experienced in our various faith communities the reality that we still have the Scriptures—at least some of them. The Scriptures have been tucked away in our people's memory. Allow me to share one personal story. Last week in my own local church, an elderly gentleman stood and recited Psalm 119; yes, all one hundred and seventy-six verses, from memory. It took some time, of course."

Dr. Westbrook chuckled and wiped a tear away, as did many in the gathering. "The impact of his oral rendition upon our church was nothing short of amazing—as verse after verse of that beautifully-crafted, acrostic poem celebrated the Word of God. This story, and many others like it, has led to our gathering you here today. Our purpose is to discover those among our various congregations and communions who have memorized portions of the Word of God. Our anxious hope is that collectively among all our friends and followers we may find that the entire Bible is committed to memory. The Committee summoned you here—and again, we are so grateful you have come on such short notice—to ask you to survey those whom you lead in order to discover what portion of the Bible they have committed to memory.

"We have created a web site where you can report what you discover—the address for this site and instructions on how to report your findings will be passed out to you at the door on your way out. We will monitor your findings and hopefully before long we will be able to assemble a team of people who together have the whole Bible committed to memory. Undoubtedly this will be quite a large team, yet, if it does in fact exist, a great relief will come to thousands of people in our region knowing that the Bible, through memory and orality, is still accessible. So, please report to the web site anyone you know who has even the smallest portion of the Bible memorized and who is willing to be counted among the team. Thank you."

A hopeful sigh and then a collective buzz went up from the assembly as they turned to each other and began to share with each other about people they knew who had memorized parts of the Bible.

Someone said, "Wow, what if all of the Bible is captured in the memories of some people right here in West Michigan?"

"Yeah, but how are we going to get those who have the Bible memorized together?" someone else asked.

Another voice added, "I think the Committee of Concern will help us. And surely the web site idea will be an asset in the process."

Someone else said, "Just imagine. People of every age, race, and gender will be needed in order to get the entire Bible spoken. No barriers, no exceptions. This could be monumental!"

As the auditorium of scholars continued to excitedly chatter among themselves, Dr. Westbrook turned to the consortium of scholars sitting behind her on the stage and smiled. This was exactly what the Committee of Concern wanted to happen. Dr. Johnson settled back in his chair and watched and listened. This was an answer to prayer in the making.

Steve Roberts, sitting in the far back left corner of the seminary auditorium, marveled at the excitement being generated as the scholars swapped stories. Gathering those who have memorized the Word; what an idea! Steve wondered if some of the folks in his church, like Anne Cook for instance, might end up being in the regional oral communication group. He met gazes with Dr. Johnson and smiled.

○ ○ ○

NOVEMBER 24

Customers bustled in and out of Kaffehaus, a popular coffee shop in the mall near Three Rivers Community Church. Luci Dykstra sat in a quiet booth in a corner away from the rush and noise, and thought back over the past five weeks.

She had been alarmed by the disappearance of the Bible and had searched out a church to find some answers. Her search had led her to TRCC where she had been surprised to see the large crowd that had gathered. She hadn't been the only newcomer that Sunday morning. The pastor, Steve, had been honest about his own fears and concerns about the empty pages in the Bible and his discomfort had somehow comforted Luci in an odd sort of way. *I'm not the only one weirded out by all this*, she had thought.

What had touched Luci the most that morning was when Steve had the church recite Psalm 23. It had been years since those words had come from Luci's mouth, but they had come nonetheless. And with the words had come tears. Luci then and there had decided to come back to TRCC again. She had been convinced that she felt God in the people.

After the service Luci had been in the foyer looking at some material about Christianity that the church was giving away. For free. Tracy Myers had seen her there and had come over and introduced herself.

"Hi, I'm Tracy. What's your name?"

Luci had looked around for a way to slip out, but realized she couldn't without insulting this stranger.

"I'm Luci."

"Is this your first time at Three Rivers Church, Luci?"

"Yeah. I came 'cause I was wondering what was happening to the Bible."

"Aren't we all wondering?" Tracy had laughed.

Luci had smiled and said, "Yeah, I guess so. Even the pastor is wondering. That really surprised me."

"Yeah, I like him because he's very honest with us. No religious Christianese from him."

"Christianese?"

"Yeah, Christianese. You know, special language just for the Christian 'insiders'—to keep the 'outsiders' out. Steve let's us know that with God we're all 'outsiders.' God in his great love became an 'outsider' like all of us. That outsider-God's name is Jesus. The reason Jesus came—God in the flesh—was to invite us in. Whoever wants to can be 'in' with God. When we fall in love with Jesus and follow him and his way, we discover a whole new way of life. We become part of a whole new people."

Tracy had fallen quiet, as she noticed the booklet about Christianity that Luci was holding in her hand.

"Hey, Luci, what are your plans right now? Do you want to grab some coffee at Kaffehaus and talk some more about all of this?"

Luci had hesitated, thinking that she really didn't want to get tied up with this girl, but something inside had her nudged her to agree. "Yes, I'd like to do that."

The two, though very different in background and at two very different places in their spiritual journeys, had hit it off right away. They were now meeting for coffee each Sunday, and this was their fifth time to meet at Kaffehaus.

Tracy sat Luci's latte down on the table and then slid into her seat. "Sorry it took me so long, but they accidentally made mine a decaf, so I had to wait while they made another one. Anyway, back to what you were saying . . . about Wayne."

"Yeah. Well, it's just that he thinks that the Bible's disappearance is no big deal. He's actually thankful, he says, because the Bible has been the cause of so many wars and deaths. He throws in my face the crusades, the ridiculous witch hunts, the murder of thousands of Native Americans by those claiming to be 'Christian' leaders. I just don't know, Tracy, but I can't be that harsh about it. I grew up believing in God and the Bible, and when the Bible disappeared, I felt like God disappeared. Do you know what I mean?"

Tracy responded, "I think I do, Luci. I told you that my parents are missionaries in Irian Jaya. When their work on the Gospel of John disappeared, it caused a crisis of faith for my dad. He just couldn't understand why God would allow that to happen. He's doing better now, but for a few weeks there I thought he was going to reject God . . . just throw out Christianity. And he's a missionary!"

"What's helped your dad?" Luci asked with genuine concern, hoping that what had helped Tracy's dad could help her, too.

"Dad said that what helped him the most was a letter from Dr. Harold Johnson. The Johnsons go to our church, and my dad had Dr Johnson as a teacher years ago. Dr. Johnson wrote him saying that it was important to realize that God and God's Word are two distinct realities. And just because the Bible disappeared, doesn't mean that God disappeared. That idea helped my dad turn some kind of corner in his soul."

Luci looked off into the distance, and Tracy could tell that she was thinking deeply about her life.

Luci said, "You know, when I come to Three Rivers and Steve has someone or all of us recite a Bible passage from memory, I feel that God is very much alive. It's like the Bible takes on a voice, God's voice, a living voice that we can hear and respond to. When I am with Wayne, and I look at the blank pages in my Bible, I get scared and begin to feel all alone again."

"Wow, Luci, that's amazing. Maybe God wants us to hear him alive in the voices of one another. We'll have to think about that. I do think Dr. Johnson is on to something when he urges us to separate the living God and the book from God. While they both are very valuable to us, we mustn't get them confused with each other."

"I wonder how many people are like me?" Luci mused aloud, "Thinking that the Bible and God are inseparable . . . like Siamese twins?"

"Probably millions, Luci. That would be my guess. That's why I think it's fantastic that Bible scholars and pastors and priests and rabbis are gathering people who have parts of the Bible memorized. I heard the other day that there are major cities on every continent now where whole portions of the Bible can be heard. Paradoxically, it seems that God is more alive and at work in the world without the Bible here. God has given us the Bible and now it's out of print . . . except for a few pages. Yet God is still alive and well and doing some amazing things. I can't explain it. It's sort of mysterious, don't you think?"

"I saw something on the news about people meeting to hear the Bible spoken. All kinds of people, young and old, are meeting each other and discovering that together they have whole parts of the Bible committed to memory."

"What is so amazing to me about that is thinking of the chapters in the Old Testament that are nothing more than lists of names—'chronicles' they are called. That's where our Jewish rabbi friends have really helped us!" Tracy smiled.

Both girls sat quietly for awhile.

"Luci, take your napkin and a pen. Try to write, 'God was reconciling the world to himself in Christ, not counting people's sins against them.'"

Luci did as Tracy suggested and even as she wrote the words down, they both marveled at how they just as quickly disappeared. Right before their eyes the whole scary reality of a world without the written Word of God was verified.

"That is spooky," Luci said quietly as she watched the last of the words vanish.

"I know, Luci, it *is*. But what I said and what you wrote is still very true. God loves you so much, Luci. All you've been through . . . with your parents . . . with churches . . . with Wayne . . . with life itself—none of it can stop God from loving you. Luci, I think God deeply honors your hunger for him."

"Do you really think so, Tracy?"

"I know so, friend."

● ● ●

JANUARY 3

The TV in the Cook's family room blared, "This is *ABC World News Tonight* with Carl Wilson."

"Anne, the news is on."

"I'm coming, I'm coming."

"Good evening. Our top story tonight is about Jared Draper, a fourteen-year-old from Sioux Falls, South Dakota, who is autistic. What is remarkable about Jared is that he has the entire New Testament memorized.

"As you know, the Jewish and Christian world is still recovering from the unexplainable disappearance of the Bible. Because there are no written Scriptures, in fact, no recorded media whatsoever of the Holy Bible, Jews and Christians who have memorized segments of the Bible are gathering at specific cities in the world to form oral communities in which the words of the Bible are preserved and shared. Jared is among them, right here in the heartland of our country, and he is a marvel to those who see and hear him.

"Let's go to Wendy Lawson who is live in Sioux Falls."

"Hello, Carl. I am here with Jared Draper and his parents, Carl and Lydia, in their home in Sioux Falls. Carl operates the Farm Feed and Supply Store here in town, and Lydia is a substitute teacher in the local elementary school. Let me ask you first, Lydia, will you tell us more about Jared's remarkable memory?"

"Well, as you know, Jared is autistic, and we discovered early on that he could remember almost word-for-word anything that was said to him. When he was younger we would play the New Testament on tape to Jared at night as he would go to sleep. Little did we know how valuable Jared's memorization of those tapes would end up being." Wendy turned her attention to Carl Draper.

"Carl, you must be amazed at Jared's sudden popularity with people of faith. His name is becoming very well known. How do you feel about Jared's sudden value to those who want to hear the New Testament?"

"Well, Wendy, we, too, are 'people of faith' as you say, and we have always believed God had a special purpose for Jared. We weren't sure what that purpose was, but now we know. Jared's been asked to meet with lots of very smart people, some were scholars from Oxford, Aberdeen, and even Moscow. So many have come and they just want Jared to recite portions of the New Testament to them. Folks are amazed that a fourteen-year-old boy, who some would call 'handicapped', can flawlessly repeat the entire New Testament."

Wendy turned and looked happily into the camera. "Well, now let's talk to Jared."

The camera panned to the end of the sofa and locked in on the somewhat chubby, yet sober, face of Jared Draper. He had big, brown eyes and spiky, brown hair. Wendy sat next to him and, glancing at the camera, asked, "Jared, how do you like all the attention you've been getting?"

"I, I, uh, like it a lot. I am . . . am happy to help people."

"How do you help them, Jared?"

"I, um, I tell them the Word of God. I tell them the New Testament."

"Will you tell us some of the New Testament, Jared?"

"Sure, I, I will. Wha . . . wha . . . what do you want me to say?"

Wendy had prepared herself in case Jared asked her this question. "How about Jesus' Sermon on the Mount? Matthew 5–7."

Jared gave a slight nod and began to articulate in a clear and unhindered voice the text of Matthew 5:

> Now when he saw the crowds, he went up on a mountainside and sat down. His disciples came to him, and he began to teach them saying:
>
> Blessed are the poor in spirit,
>   for theirs is the kingdom of heaven.
> Blessed are those who mourn,
>   for they will be comforted.
> Blessed are the meek,
>   for they will inherit the earth.
> Blessed are those who hunger and thirst for righteousness,
>   for they will be filled.
> Blessed are the merciful,
>   for they will be shown mercy . . . .

As Jared's voice continued steadily on, Wendy stepped away from the couch and delivered her closing lines.

"Carl, Jared Draper is a sweet and remarkably gifted child. He's reciting for us Jesus' famous sermon even as I sign off. This is Wendy Lawson for *ABC News*, in Sioux Falls, South Dakota."

The TV screen filled with a head shot of Carl Wilson.

"Remarkable report, Wendy." Carl said, addressing her through the monitor. "Jared Draper is an amazing young man."

Then turning to look into camera one, he said, "We'll be back in a moment with more news. Stay tuned."

Ben looked at Anne. Both of them had tears in their eyes.

"Unbelievable, Ben. That young boy has the entire New Testament memorized. Anyone on this planet who needs to know something from the New Testament just needs to contact Jared."

"I was thinking the same thing. Here's this autistic boy who has become a champion to Christians everywhere. I bet even more scholars will be coming to him now."

"Yeah," Anne paused thoughtfully. "I wonder how many more gifted children there are who have huge sections of the Bible memorized. Think of it. Children, of all people. Unbelievable."

"'And a little child will lead them,'" Ben whispered in wonder.

"What did you say?"

"'A little child' . . . 'The last will be first.'"

○ ○ ○

JANUARY 25

Karla and Hank Myers tossed their suitcases and carry-on bags on the bed in their Tokyo hotel room. After spending seventeen hours in the air—first Jim Samsa's little Cessna to Nabire, then from there to the international airport in Jakarta, and on from there to Tokyo—they were exhausted. They were on their way back to the States. The loss of their years of work on the Gospel of John had taken such a toll on them spiritually and emotionally that they felt like they needed a break. Their mission leaders had granted them a spontaneous six-month furlough to fly home and see their daughter, Tracy, and visit other family, friends, and supporting churches. An added blessing was getting to make this little stop over in Japan to see Rick and Staci Nolan—good friends of theirs from missions school.

"I've got the shower first," laughed Karla. "I can't see Staci and Rick looking like this!"

"You look great . . . ravishing even, hon," Hank said.

"Yeah, but only to you. I'll hurry."

With three minutes to spare Hank and Karla took the elevator down from their eleventh- floor room. The hotel, near the airport, was westernized and felt like sheer luxury to the Myers who had been working in the mountains of Irian Jaya. The elevator door opened, and as they stepped into the lobby, they heard the boom of a familiar voice.

"There they are! Hank and Karla, the couple most likely to succeed and to breed! How are you guys!"

It was Rick's deep, happy bass voice thundering across the hotel lobby.

"Rick, stop that!" Staci scolded in a mortified whisper. "You'll embarrass them to death."

They greeted each other and hugged, all the while Rick was slapping Hank on the back and joking around like they had in missions school.

"Gosh, Rick, I don't think we succeeded and we didn't breed much, either." Hank said "We've got Tracy living in Michigan. That's it. And you've heard about what happened to our Gospel of John work."

"Yeah, we heard, Hank. That's tragic. The whole thing with the Bible disappearing has thrown a monkey-wrench into a lot of missions' work. Some friends of ours in the Philippines, the Chapkos, who serve with the Bible League were sent home to Montana. There are no Bibles to distribute. And, do you remember Phil and Brenda from missions' school? The Bible school in Ghana where they teach has been shut down. They returned to Oklahoma just a month ago. But, hey! Tonight's a night for fun. Staci and I are going to take you to dinner at a neat restaurant where some amazing things are happening. Ya' game?"

"You betcha! We're starving. Let's go."

The taxi took them through the streets of Tokyo where the buildings were lit up with dazzling lights for miles. Parts of the city were as bright at night as the heart of Las Vegas. All this modernization and light was overwhelming and foreign to Karla and Hank, but it felt "like home" to Rick and Staci. Soon the taxi stopped at the entrance of *Jyu*, a popular Japanese cuisine restaurant specializing in seafood.

"Here's the place! You guys are going to love it. And tonight Staci and I are treating you two."

"Why, Rick, you don't have to do that," Karla said.
"I know we don't have to, but we want to. 'Nuff said, okay?"
"Okay."

The food was everything they expected. Karla had tempura shrimp and Hank stuck with one of his non-seafood favorites, *tonkatsu*: Japanese fried pork. Rick and Staci both ordered red snapper. The rice and vegetables, the tea and bread—everything was mouth-wateringly delicious.

The two couples shared stories, caught up on how their kids were doing, and talked about other friends doing missionary work under the unusual conditions without written Scriptures.

"Hey, I said there was something special about this place, and I meant more than just the good food. Are we finished with the meal?" Rick asked.

"I am stuffed," said Hank.

"I couldn't eat another thing," Karla said.

"Me neither," echoed Staci.

"Then follow me."

Rick got up and led them behind a beautifully painted screen to a side room, where the arrangement of exotic lounge chairs, couches, smoke-colored glass coffee tables and end tables created a surreal sense of peace and quiet. Small bamboo trees in decorative clay pots graced several corners of the room. The recessed lights were low making the room look like it was washed in the colors of a soft setting sun. Karla mused, *You would think you're still outside.* A steady Japanese voice could be heard over the speakers.

The Myers and Nolans found some seats. A waiter brought them more cups and a pot of tea.

"Rick, what is this place?" Hank asked.

"Just listen," whispered Rick, and nodded toward the front of the room.

Sitting on a stool was a young Japanese woman holding a microphone. She was speaking softly into it and her voice was carried throughout the sitting room. As she spoke, she often smiled.

"What's she doing? What's she saying?" Karla whispered to Staci.

"She's reciting Scripture. It's the book of Romans right now, and I think she started by reciting the Gospel of Luke. I think I faintly heard her when we first arrived."

"What!" Hank exclaimed, working hard to keep his voice quiet.

"That's right, Hank. She's simply reciting the Scriptures. This part of the restaurant is called a Bible Listening Room. They are all over Japan, and from what I've heard they are springing up in cities all over the world. People can come and just hear the Bible."

"You've got to be kidding!" Hank responded incredulously.

"No, thank God, I'm not kidding. The Japanese authorities have allowed these listening rooms out of respect for Jewish and Christian religion. Sometimes the Old Testament books are recited and sometimes, like tonight, New Testament books. There are Japanese people who have memorized the Scriptures, and they are allowed to recite. It's very orderly, and just look around; it's unbelievably received."

Hank and Karla were stunned at the many attentive faces of the people sitting and listening. The young woman's voice was soft, yet clear, and it carried a tone of undeniable strength.

"She's reciting the end of Romans 12 now," Rick whispered.

In clear Japanese, the listeners heard:

> *Live in harmony with one another. Do not be proud, but be willing to associate with people of low position. Do not be conceited.*
>
> *Do not repay anyone evil for evil. Be careful to do what is right in the eyes of everybody. If it is possible, as far as it depends on you, live at peace with everyone. Do not take revenge, my friends, but leave room for God's wrath, for it is written: "It is mine to avenge; I will repay," says the Lord. On the contrary:*
>
> *"If your enemy is hungry, feed him;*
> *if he is thirsty, give him something to drink.*
>
> *In doing this, you will heap burning coals on his head."*
> *Do not be overcome by evil, but overcome evil with good.*

○ ○ ○

JANUARY 27

Rabbi Jakob Spielman took a sip of water from the bottle in front of him and then excitedly addressed the Committee of Concern gathered in a small conference room at Grand Rivers Theological Seminary.

"My friends, we have seen marvelous things happening in these months since we asked people who have committed the Word of God to memory to gather. I received a message from a friend of mine at the Hebrew University in Jerusalem that fifteen Jewish men have been gathered and with just this small group, almost all of the Hebrew Bible is memorized. One man alone knows all of Moses—the Pentateuch—and the Psalms. Another is a ninety-seven-year-old Talmudic scholar, a survivor of Auschwitz, who knows many of what you call 'the history' books of the Old Testament—Joshua, Judges, Ruth, Nehemiah, and Ezra. However, Samuel, Kings, and Chronicles are not covered . . . yet." He smiled and continued, "This is simply too amazing to me. The other men know some of these same books, as well as many of the Writings and Prophets—Ezekiel, Habakkuk, and Nahum are the only prophets not covered. And, hear this, my friends. They discovered a brilliant Jewish student who has a photographic memory and who knows all of the New Testament *in Hebrew* except for the books of Acts, Hebrews, and the Revelation of St. John. He learned it because he wanted to be able to dialogue with Christians about their faith in Yeshua of Nazareth. He is also one of the fifteen!"

Father Demitri Kassius grinned with sheer wonder. Then he spoke up in a soft, yet radiant voice, "Rabbi Spielman, I am so grateful to hear your story about the findings of the Scriptures in Hebrew. And I think we are all aware of the young boy, Jared Draper, an autistic child in South Dakota, who has the entire New Testament in English memorized, yes?"

Those on the council all nodded. "Well, my friends, my uncle who is a Greek Orthodox priest in St. Petersburg, Russia, called me and told me that they have found an old woman, a *babushka* of seventy-two years of age, who has all the epistles of the New Testament memorized in Greek. It is somewhat faulty Greek, but nevertheless, a treasure to our people and to the world, yes?"

There was an extended pause as the scholars marveled at the momentum developing and the discoveries unfolding about the enduring presence of God's Word on the planet.

Dr. Katherine Westbrook gently broke the silence.

"My friends, our web site has been receiving data from around the world. There are, at this moment, eighty-six regions around the globe where most of the Bible is accessible in the memory of groups of people. We have the Bible in English, almost all of it in Hebrew, Japanese, German, French, and with the *babushka* in St. Petersburg, we now have a good portion of the Greek New Testament.

"An unforeseen development spinning out of these groups is something being called "mission memory seminars" or MMS's where those who have memorized the portions of the Bible are helping others, orally, to memorize the parts they know. These new carriers of the Bible then spread out and help develop new regions where the Bible can be made orally available. These MMS's are being supported by many very wealthy Christians and Jews and religious foundations. It's uncanny, unbelievable really, the amount of money being given to help spread the Word of God from mouth-to-mouth.

"Some groups, passionate about keeping God's Word alive in our present unusual situation, have already formed 24-7 recitations of the entire Bible. Others are being invited by radio stations and given free airtime to simply speak the Scriptures on an ongoing basis. Bible Listening Rooms are opening in cities around the world where people can come in and listen to the Scriptures being recited. I'm having a hard time keeping up with the reports incessantly coming in.

"What is amazing is that all sorts of people—old, young, rich, poor, academics and impaired, business teams, and whole families—are flocking into these listening rooms. The impact of all this is nothing short of absolutely miraculous. Others, who are monitoring the feedback are as astounded as I am by this global, unexplainable interest in the Word of God simply recited—not explained, not sermonized, not analyzed—just spoken 'as is.'"

Dr. Harold Johnson raised his hand. He had been thinking about the astounding cooperation of Southern Baptists with mainline denominations—Lutherans, Methodists, Episcopalians, and

Presbyterians. Southern Baptists are not known for ecumenical fraternizing. Some Southern Baptist leaders were even cooperating with Catholic priests and Jewish Rabbis. The loss of the Scriptures was compelling denominational walls to come down and causing meaningful relationships to be built. Evangelicals were serving with Pentecostals; Vineyard churches were mixing it up with Bible churches and Christian Reformed churches. Catholics, Protestants, and Jews were collaborating to revive the Scriptures orally.

"Yes, Harry," Katherine responded.

"Many of my colleagues are observing a marvelous change in Christian leaders, theologians, and pastors. The current crisis has eroded much of the infighting, divisiveness, and arguing over minor and obscure doctrinal intricacies. While admitting that there are differences—valid and, perhaps, valuable differences—in the global Christian community, they have realized that old doctrinal divides are not as important as the challenge to keep the word of God active and known on the planet. Keeping the word of God alive in an oral way has generated a remarkable unity and cooperation among many who were theological adversaries. Honoring the gift of the Bible itself has tempered so many unnecessary schisms among so many who truly long to love God and love people. This emerging and expanding unity is a phenomenon in itself.

"It's almost like what happens when children are fighting over a favorite toy and the parent takes the toy away. I'm not saying God is actually the One who took the Bible away, but its absence has sure squelched a lot of childish squabbling in the church at large. The unified mission to reclaim the Bible in oral form has overridden so many factions. People are linking arms and working together for a greater cause than sectarian and theological peculiarities." Harold paused, reflecting on the miracles he had just reported.

Katherine spoke, continuing Harold's line of thought. "It seems that the grand Story of the Bible got lost in all the tedious footnotes of the various expressions within Christianity. Now it seems that the recovery of God's Story is the most important aim as the Bible is being recited worldwide. I am amazed. But I have to admit that my amazement is in a sense, at the same time, a shame, an indictment of my own theological self-absorption. Why did it take something like this to get us—Jewish, Catholic, Orthodox, and Protestant leaders—united around something bigger than ourselves and our views?"

Demitri nodded in agreement. "We have enjoyed an unusual unity over these past months, it is true. But let's be gut-level honest, there are still *deep differences* here around this table. Jews and Christians have very different beliefs about Jesus of Nazareth. Protestants and Catholics still need to think through some of the Reformation issues and beliefs about canonicity and the Virgin Mary. But all of us are recipients of revelation from God—the Holy Scriptures. We Christians are deeply indebted to the Jews and are inheritors of God's love and promises to them. Yahweh, blessed be his name, is our God, and yes, we believe that Yeshua of Nazareth is Yahweh incarnate. Protestants and Catholics and the Orthodox affirm a Trinitarian God; that human beings are infinitely valuable as 'image-bearers' of that God; and that salvation is through Jesus Christ alone. But back to the differences. The question amidst these differences is: Can we *love* each other deeply from the heart, since we claim that God loves each person that he has created? Can we learn to say, 'I think you're wrong on that issue' and do it in a way that preserves the value and dignity of our fellow human beings?"

The others shook their heads in agreement.

Harold spoke up again. "I, as you all know, am a Christian Protestant and am theologically conservative. You are my friends. You are Jewish and Catholic and Orthodox. I will listen to you and respect you and your views even while I disagree with you—strongly at times. You have listened with great respect to me and to those like me. At the end of the day, the question is not: Did I convince you to believe like me? I agree with Demitri and I emphasize that it must become a worldwide value. The real question is: Do we love each other as God-created *human beings* from the heart?

"The present crisis and the way people of all persuasions are rallying to meet the crisis have taught me a valuable lesson. Without the Bible, without God, we don't know the value of each human being. Even when we had the Bible, we lost vision of the value of each human being by our global, incessant religious fighting. With Bible in hand, we defamed fellow image-bearers of God. We vandalized each other with the word of God and when we did, we desecrated the very creations of God. For this I feel ashamed and will live to affirm the value of each person no matter their religious beliefs."

"Harry, my own heart is stirred and warmed by your confession. Can we be content to let God be the Judge of our beliefs? Can we find a way to love one another, even when we disagree deeply about the things of the soul and of the life to come? I know that Yeshua of Nazareth declared the *Shema* to be the greatest commandment and that the next greatest was to also love your neighbor as yourself. To *that* teaching of Yeshua of Nazareth I can and shall agree. Blessed be God, the Maker of heaven and earth and all of mankind. What is the great Story of the Bible if not the Story of Adonai-Elohim's great love?"

A holy silence rested upon the group.

"Gentlemen, let's close this meeting in prayer," Katherine quietly suggested.

● ● ●

Wayne took another bite of pizza and washed it down with a swallow of beer. He was tired and really didn't want to have *this* conversation with Luci, but she kept talking.

"I've found hope, Wayne, real hope and I think you will, too. With all the confusion and fear in the world, I've found a family, a Christian community that cares about me. The people at Three Rivers Church took me in and listened to me and reacquainted me with God. It was like I met God again for the first time. I was introduced to a God who is truly here and really and deeply cares about us, even though the Bible is gone."

"Listen, Luc', I don't want to hear about 'church.' Any church. I don't need 'God' taking care of me. I don't need a Bible. I'll take care of me, thank you."

"But what are you living for, Wayne? Why do you get up in the morning? Where is your life headed?"

"I'm living for me. And I'm doing just fine. I don't need to be heading anywhere to have a good time."

"A good time? That's what you think life is about? C'mon, Wayne, you're worth more than that. Life can be so much more than just a good time."

Wayne ripped off another big bite of pizza and chewed, getting more angry with what he thought was a lecture from Luci.

"Just leave me alone, Luc'! I mean it." He spit bits of pizza out as he shouted at her. "I'm doing okay, dammit, and I don't need a sermon from you. What's wrong with you anyway? You got religion and now you're all over me. Well, I don't need it and I don't want it. Where's the Luci that used to have a good time?"

"She grew up, I guess. I'm moving on, Wayne. I do care about you, yet I have to confess that what I thought was love before was just fear. I was afraid to be alone and I thought being with you was 'love.' Actually, it was fear trying to find some hope. I was using you to find some security, just as you were using me to have sex. Admit it."

She paused.

"Do you love me, Wayne?"

"Hey, don't get all philosophical on me, Luc'. I want to be with you."

"Really?"

"Yeah, really."

"Do you care about what I think? I mean really think?"

"Of course, I do."

"Then come with me to Three Rivers on Sunday. The people there are an important part of me now and shape what I think is important these days."

"Oh, c'mon, Luc', you know I can't do that. I really don't want to."

"But you said you really care about me and what I think."

Wayne crammed the remaining stub of pizza crust into his mouth and gazed past Luci. He couldn't look her in the eyes. He felt confused and angry. He felt trapped.

As if she were reading his mind, Luci said, "I don't want to box you in, Wayne. I really care about you, but there are some things in my life now that I care more about. This is the last time I will be with you. But know the door is always open. If you want to meet me again, meet me at Three Rivers."

"Oh c'mon, Luc'. I've missed you . . . ah, I mean, the old you, the before-I-met-Jesus you. Can't we go back to the good time? Huh?"

Luci got up and walked past him to the door. Wayne stared at her, but didn't really see her. In his blanket of self-absorption, all he saw was his own pitiful loneliness.

"Bye," she whispered weakly, opened the door and walked out.

"I'll be just fine," he muttered to himself in the silence that crowded in close around him. "I'll take care of me."

Staring into nothingness, Wayne felt the chilling embrace of isolation.

○ ○ ○

FEBRUARY 1

The setting sun painted a beautiful orange and purple sky on a cool, clear evening as folks arrived for the weekly home group meeting at Steve and Betsy Roberts' home.

Betsy was at the door welcoming her guests.

"Tracy and Luci, it's so good to see you two. Here, let me take that."

Luci handed Betsy a pan of brownies freshly baked just before she and Tracy had left her new apartment.

"Thanks, Betsy. Those should be good with your coffee a little later on."

The two girls made their way to the living room and sat down just as Betsy turned around to answer the door again. Harold and Marty Johnson were already comfortably settled on the couch. Tracy and Luci and the Johnsons greeted each other with friendly embraces.

Jim and Nancy DeLano came in and hugged and greeted the Roberts, the Johnsons and Tracy and Luci.

"We've got a surprise for you all!" Nancy announced with a big grin.

A knock on the door was quickly followed with it opening before Betsy got to it. There standing with their own big grins stood Hank and Karla.

Betsy shrieked and said, "Hank, Karla, what a wonderful surprise! When did you get into town? We didn't expect you until tomorrow!"

Karla answered, "Some things changed in our itinerary, and so we ended up getting in late last night. We called our darling Tracy to let her know we were in. Nancy, Jim, and Tracy came and met us at the airport, but we told them to keep it a secret—we wanted to surprise you. We fell exhausted into bed at Jim and Nancy's."

Steve jumped up and greeted Hank with a bear hug.

"It is so good to see you, Hank. Oh, Karla, we're glad you two made it home safely. I bet you're tired."

"Jet lag can be tough," Hank agreed, "but we slept well last night. We've been running on adrenaline since we left Nabire. I expect a crash is just around the corner . . . but not tonight. It's so good to be here, Steve. It's so good to see all of you. And thanks, punkin', for keeping the secret."

Tracy smiled at her Dad and watched happily as her parents settled into the room, surrounded by the sounds of joyful reunion. She had been so worried about the toll the disappearance of their translation work had had on them, especially on her father. But in the midst of their tearful reunion at the airport last night, something in their eyes made her feel that somehow everything was going to be okay. Now she was sure of it."

"Dad, Mom, I want you to meet my friend Luci. Luci, this is my dad, Hank, and my mom, Karla."

"It's good to meet you, Mr. and Mrs. Myers. Tracy has really been a good friend to me during these scary times we're in. I was really troubled by the disappearance of the Bible. But Tracy has helped . . . and Pastor Steve and all these folks here have."

Karla replied, "Oh, Luci, we've all been troubled. This is like nothing in human history. We're finding we not only need the Bible, we need one another as well. It's a delight to meet you."

Steve Roberts looked around the room. *So much is happening in the lives of the folks here. So much is happening in the church and in the world. To be alive at this time in history is unsettling that's for sure, but it is also very exciting, almost invigorating.* With a happy sigh, he addressed the group.

"Thanks, everyone, for coming tonight. We are especially surprised to see Hank and Karla. Welcome home, you two."

"Amen to that!" Tracy shouted and there were chuckles all around.

"Ben and Anne . . . the Cooks, are going to be late." Steve continued. "Ben was bogged down at his office and couldn't get away. Luci, it's so good to see you again tonight."

"Thanks, Pastor Steve. I'm very glad to be here, too."

"Well, let's get started. Let me open our gathering with prayer."

After Steve's heart-felt prayer, he asked Hank and Karla to give a brief update of their trip home and how they were feeling about their recent loss.

"Sure, Hank, go ahead."

Hank began by reporting to the group about eating at the *Jyu* restaurant with the Nolans and about the Bible Listening Room. Karla spoke as well, telling about the beauty of the reading and the attentiveness of the patrons. They reported their amazement at such a reality and at how the Bible was being respected all over Japan.

". . . and Rick Nolan said that similar 'listening rooms' are appearing in major cities around the world," Hank concluded.

"That's true," chimed in Harold Johnson. "The regional Committee of Concern met a few days back and Katherine Westbrook, our chairperson and a scholar from Toledo, reported the same thing. It's nothing short of miraculous—this global interest in the Bible."

"Yeah, it's the Bible 'unplugged,'" Luci called out.

The group laughed.

"Really unplugged . . . unpreached . . . uncommented on. Who would have thunk it?" laughed Steve.

The doorbell rang.

"That must be Ben and Anne. They'll be disappointed they missed your report, Hank."

Betsy got up to answer the door. When the Cooks came in, everyone relived the joy of being reunited. Anne gave Karla a big hug and Ben and Hank slapped each other a high five. Laughter was the chorus of the evening.

When the group settled into their places, Steve asked that they recite the Lord's Prayer together. The group got silent, then Steve's voice led out, and others quickly joined in:

Our Father in heaven,
hallowed be your name,
your kingdom come,
your will be done
  on earth as it is in heaven.
Give us today our daily bread.
Forgive us our debts,
  as we also have forgiven our debtors.
And lead us not into temptation,
  but deliver us from the evil one
for yours is the kingdom and the power
and the glory forever. Amen.

During the prayer Luci's eyes filled with tears and by the end she was softly weeping.

"Why are you crying, Luci?" Steve tenderly asked.

"Oh, I don't know. Lots of reasons I guess. The sound of the words of that prayer, the love I feel in this room, and the ache I have for my boyfriend, Wayne."

She paused. "Ex-boyfriend, actually."

Luci wiped her eyes and looked around the room. "I left Wayne. I told him I would not see him again unless he met me at Three Rivers. I told him that something more important is in my life than living with him. He is so resistant to God . . . and church . . . and now to me. This whole disappearance of the Bible is no big deal to him. He says he's going to take care of himself, yet I know he is so lonely."

She dropped her head and began to cry into a kleenex.

Harold Johnson spoke up gently. "Luci, we admire you for caring for Wayne. You've actually done him a huge favor. He needs to know that there are some things more valuable in life than you being with him. Maybe God will use Wayne's loneliness to open a door into his life, but I stress the word 'maybe' . . . we can't say for sure."

"I know," Luci sniffed. "It's just that I thought he really cared about me. He says he does, but he doesn't want to talk with me about the hope I've found in Jesus. He won't let me talk about it. He thinks I'm giving him a sermon."

Tracy put her arm around Luci's shoulder. "We all agree with Dr. Johnson that you have done a good thing for Wayne. And God can do even greater things in his life. We'll pray for Wayne and for you."

"Thanks," Luci sniffed again, and smiled.

Tracy led the group in a prayer for Luci and Wayne. After the "Amen" the group was quiet. Then Harold Johnson spoke up. "

"Karla and Hank, I was so excited to hear about your experiences in the Japanese restaurant. As I mentioned earlier, the regional Committee of Concern was updated on the global spontaneous expansion of these Bible Listening Rooms. Also, MMS's are being formed—mission memory seminars—to help orally pass on the Bible to those who don't have it. The way things are going, one day the oral Bible will be accessible at every point on the planet. The Bible simply being recited has become a magnet to human attention. The way Jews are showing an interest in the *New* Testament and Christians are needing the Jews for the Old Testament is uncanny. Catholic and Protestant scholars are developing a deep respect for each other as they work together to have just the Bible itself accessible. The profound Christian-Jewish, Protestant-Catholic-Orthodox cooperation has caught the attention of the Muslim world. Something truly greater than our differences is causing us to communicate with each other. While recognizing the differences, the adversarial spirit is greatly reduced in the common quest to just have the Bible. No one could have expected that such great things would come out of such a crisis. What I'm trying to say, Luci, is that God is doing some amazing things in the world . . . and at the same time he never loses sight of Wayne. We'll keep praying for him. Who knows what God might do?"

Anne Cook spoke up. "Harry, you're right about God doing amazing things these days. I'm part of the regional MMS, a group that as of now is composed of forty-two people and we have all of the Bible except 1 and 2 Chronicles, Ezekiel, Acts, and Revelation covered. But we have some leads on some people who may have those books committed to memory. I am part of a subgroup that has all the Psalms committed to memory. So, right here in the Grand Rivers region we have all of the Bible except for five books. In such a short time!"

"That is amazing," said Luci. "I was so afraid when the news first started reporting that the Bible was disappearing. I thought that a world without a Bible would be a world without God. But it's seems to me to be just the opposite. The Bible has come alive to me. Its absence made me want it all the more. Isn't that just crazy?"

Harold answered, "Luci, I think we—and by 'we' I mean scholars and leaders in the Christian world—have observed something that is counterintuitive. The absence of the Bible has in itself created a great hunger for it in the lives of people. Why is this? We're still trying to put words to it. Is it because the Bible is a world renown, religious book? Is it because it is the revered writings of both Jews and Christians? Is the interest generated simply by the fact that it has disappeared, like you have said, Luci? We just don't know."

"Yeah, but Dr. Johnson," responded Luci, "it's not just because the words of the Bible are gone. It's something deeper that I can't quite express. It's like an ache, a fear, a yearning leapt up in me the first time I heard the news reporter speak the phrase, '. . . a world without the Bible.' When I heard that phrase I was scared and, and it was like a still small voice inside me saying right then, 'What has God said to you in the Bible?' and I really wanted the answer to that question. I wondered if when the Bible closes, does God stop speaking. Is God's voice locked into the pages of a book? And if the book closes or disappears does God become mute? Does that make sense?"

Harold Johnson leaned back in his chair and looked at Luci and said, "You are the living paradox that is being reported around the globe. With no Bible, there is a hunger for it. We're in a virtual famine of the written Word. What you tell us would explain the attention to the Bible reading in a Tokyo restaurant, a Paris hotel lobby, a Chicago airport waiting area, an Australian library room, and a Kiev theatre. Around the globe there seems to be a mysterious hunger to hear words from the Bible. We've gotten word that the initial swagger of the Muslims reported by that scholar on *Lawrence Kingsley Live* has dissipated. Muslim leaders, who boasted that they still have their Koran, are stunned by the worldwide interest in hearing the Jewish and Christian Bible recited. How funny is that?"

Nancy DeLano asked, "Harold, it is wonderful to hear about all these good results from the Bible's disappearance, but I'm still wondering why it disappeared in the first place. I am still so confused why God did this? And, if God didn't do it, why did he *allow* it to happen?"

Ben Cook leaned forward and jumped into the conversation.

"Nancy, Anne and I have been asking that same question—who or what is behind this mess? I remember wondering, like most people do when something really bad happens, 'Why?' or even, 'Why, God?' But I just can't believe God would do such a thing—give his word and then take it away. And if the Devil did it—like the now off-the-air-TV-preacher Randy Joe Jason taught—how did the Devil 'get permission' from God to do it?

Harold broke in, "We've discussed this before. While I'm still not sure of all of this, I can say that I used to think that same way, Ben. I believed that God had everything pre-planned. I mean *everything*. We scholars call it his eternal and partly hidden decree. God has decreed everything, including the actions of his and his people's enemies. That means all the hostility against God and against God's will has been secretly decreed by God himself. In this view it would logically follow that God has decreed war against himself. I used to believe that if anything ever happened outside God's decree—outside his will—then he would not be totally or fully sovereign. It would seem like God loses control. Even the movements of leptons have been decreed. But now I—"

"What's a lepton?" Karla interrupted.

"It's a nano-particle extremely smaller than a proton or a neutron."

"You say you *used* to believe that, Harry," Anne said. "What do you think now?"

Harold took a sip of water, closed his eyes for a few moments, opened them and continued, "Now, I am not so sure. I think that for God to decree the giving of his eternal Word and then to decree its absence makes him seem like a capricious God, playing with the human race like we were toys, mere objects. I just can't accept the view that God pre-programmed all that happens in the universe and then just hit the "execute" key. God is too loving, too relational to be reduced to an 'unblinking cosmic stare' as someone has described that kind of non-participatory God.

"Many of my fellow colleagues locally and other Christian thinkers around the world believe that human and demonic freedom is just that—true freedom. By that they mean *not all* human and demonic actions are predetermined by God's decree. This reasoning leads to the silly conclusion that Jesus the Son came to defeat and correct what God—the Three-in-One—has decreed and ordered. I just don't think that view holds up to biblical scrutiny and to the way life actually happens. "

Anne edgily countered, "But then you're saying, Harold, that God is not always or completely *in control*. Some things happen outside his will? Isn't that an assault on the power and sovereignty of God?"

"I admit, Anne, that it certainly sounds like it. But actually it seems to me that God losing control is the wrong conclusion. I don't think 'control' is that big of a deal to God. God is more about achieving a loving, glorious purpose than he is about being in meticulous control. God's ability to wisely and powerfully guide all that happens toward his wonderful purpose for the universe, rather than 'programming' it to get there actually raises the wonder and glory of God's sovereignty even higher. Our God can take the totally free, undetermined actions of humans and demons and work them into the fulfilling of his eternal purposes. So some things are certainly and eternally decreed, but not all things. God will indeed fulfill his eternal purposes. There is nothing that he cannot engage and change to bring about his desired ends. Therefore, I don't think sovereignty merely means being 'absolutely in control.'

"You and I—all of us—ask: Who is behind this, this disappearance of the Bible? Is it God? Is it Satan? Is it an anomaly of reality? I really can't tell you for certain who caused the Bible to disappear. But I can tell you this—God is doing some amazing, wonderfully unexpected things within the chaos, fear, and confusion created by the Bible's disappearance."

Luci spoke up.

"I think that one of those things that God is doing is teaching me this: God is not equal to the Bible. Like I said, I thought when the Bible vanished, God vanished. That scared me, really scared me. But I'm finding that God has given the Bible, but he is not the Bible. I'm also learning that even though the pages of the Bible are empty, that the Word of God *is still here*. It's in the kind hearts and loving actions of people like you . . . right here in this little house in Three Rivers. Just a short time ago I was just a confused girl living with her boyfriend for hope and security, but now I know God. I've seen God and heard God . . . through all of you. God is not a book. He is a person, and, and, I know God is more person than we are, ah, I mean, God is the pure, supreme personal God, but he is *God* after all. And I think that this God is alive and present and seeing and hearing *through all of you*. God is at work in the world through so many people."

After a pause she asked, "Would I even be here if the Bible had not disappeared?" She shook her head, "No, I really doubt it. So, I am living proof that God can make something good out of something bad."

The group sat in silence.

Hank spoke up, "I really hope God will do something to reach the Vahudati people. With all our work gone, I fear for their eternal well-being. I, like Harold, thought that God had everything decreed, but as I wrestled with this event in the world, I almost went mad in despair thinking, 'Why, God? Why did *you* do this?' Ultimately that was what I was left with. God is in control of all, so God is in control *of this*. It made no sense whatsoever to me." Hank had tears in his eyes, the weariness of all he'd been through leaking out and running down his face.

"Hey, we do have reason to hope," Steve assured. "Hope for Wayne, hope for the Vahudati people, Hank, and hope for this crazy planet. And Luci has reminded us of something—the hope of the world is not a book—even a holy Book. The hope of the world is the God who gave the Book, the God who came down in Jesus and lived the Book, the God now at work through people who love and speak the Book. The God of the Book seems to be rising up and expressing himself through the people of the Book."

"The way that young Japanese woman recited the book of Romans when we were in the Tokyo restaurant, you could just tell by her expression and tone of voice that she loved what she was saying," Karla remembered. "It was very precious to her. I think her love for the Bible and for the people listening to her was what was so captivating. I was captivated by it, even though I don't understand Japanese."

"I think you're exactly right, Karla," Steve replied. "The watching world is taking note of the love that Christians and Jews have for their Scriptures. The Bible is not primarily being used anymore to harangue and judge and belittle and ostracize others. It is simply being spoken and lived out by people who deeply treasure it. The Bible was meant to be a lived Book, not just a learned Book. Maybe it's as simple as 'A love letter needs to be read in a loving way.'"

With that the conversation ended and the room was quiet.

After a long silence Betsy Roberts said, "Let's have some coffee and pie and some of Tracy's delicious brownies."

4

UNSURPASSABLE

FEBRUARY 9

Nancy DeLano reached for her hot tea as she sat on the all-seasons porch at the back of their home. A gentle, cold breeze caused the powdery snow on the naked branches of the backyard maple trees to slowly lift and float to the ground. Nancy routinely came out to the porch in the late morning to read, think, and sometimes grieve over not having the chance anymore to tell children about Jesus. She had given up her Child Evangelism Fellowship club as the Bible, section by section, had disappeared. Before that happened she had often come out here to prepare her lessons, create the craft projects, and pray for each child by name. Now all of that was gone. She sipped her tea and wistfully, out of habit, reached for her Bible, now mostly blank pages between a tan leather cover.

She still was shocked every time she opened the Bible and scanned the blank pages. So often she had opened this book and read, meditated, studied, and dreamed about how to tell children about God's love for them. Now, holding the Bible just so, she fanned through the pages—animating the scattered confetti of verse numbers until they seemed to swirl and dance.

What was that?

She thought she saw something on one of the pages near the middle of her Bible. Were her eyes tricking her? She slowly fanned the pages again, and, yes, there it was a large block of text at the bottom of a page. Her hands trembling, she read:

> "The time is coming," declares the Lord,
> > "when I will make a new covenant
> > with the house of Israel
> > and with the house of Judah.
>
> It will not be like the covenant
> > I made with their forefathers
> > when I took them by the hand
> > to lead them out of Egypt,
> > because they broke my covenant,
> > though I was a husband to them,"
> > declares the Lord.
>
> "This is the covenant I will make with the house of Israel
> > after that time," declares the Lord.
> > "I will put my law in their minds
> > and write it on their hearts.
> > I will be their God,
> > and they will be my people.
>
> "No longer will a man teach his neighbor,
> > or a man his brother, saying, 'Know the Lord,'
> > because they will all know me,
> > from the least of them to the greatest,"
> > declares the Lord.
> > "For I will forgive their wickedness
> > and will remember their sins no more."

Nancy could hardly believe it. *This is Isaiah, isn't it? No, no, there at the top of my page it says "Jeremiah 31." Oh, this is the promise of the new covenant. I remember Steve preaching about this a few years ago. But wait! Why is this here in my Bible?*

She fanned through her Bible again. Those were the only words that had reappeared in her Bible. Why were these words here? She was thrilled and confused; happy and perplexed.

"I've got to tell someone about this!" she heard herself say aloud.

She reached for her cell phone and called Anne Cook. Anne answered.

"Anne! Get your Bible! You've got to get your Bible. I think there may be words in it . . . from Jeremiah! Quick, Anne!"

"Nancy, is that you? Slow down, calm down. What are you saying?"

"I found part of Jeremiah 31 in my Bible, Anne."

"What?" asked Anne excitedly.

"Yes, the words are in chapter 31. The part about the new covenant. Is it in your Bible, too, Anne?"

"Hold on while I get my Bible."

Anne ran to her bedroom and grabbed up her Bible. She quickly fumbled through the pages but didn't spot any newly appeared passages. She picked up the phone by the bed, "Are you there, Nanc'?"

"Yes, I'm here. Did you find it?"

"I'm looking. Where did you say it was?"

"It's Jeremiah 31. Look for that chapter heading. It's on a page near the middle of my Bible, Anne."

Anne laid the phone on the bed and slowly turned each page ahead of where the Bible opened. She saw chapter 28 . . . then 29 . . . 30 . . . 31 . . . There they were!

Anne ran her fingers along the lines and read them slowly. Then she read them aloud to herself.

Nancy heard her reading and began shouting through the receiver, "Hooray! You found them! You found them!"

Anne hurriedly picked the phone back up and spoke with a quivering voice. "Nancy, this is astounding. Part of the Bible is in print again. I wonder if these words have returned in print in all the Bibles in all languages of the world? This is incredible."

"Why do you think just these verses have reappeared?" Nancy asked.

"I don't know, Nanc'. Let's call Marty Johnson. Maybe she'll know. No, I tell you what. Are you free now?"

"Yes, I am."

"I'll call Marty and tell her we're coming over. Meet me at her house."

"I'll be there in ten minutes."

Nancy hung up, and holding her Bible, grabbed her car keys and headed for Marty Johnson's house. Anne did the same after a quick, excited phone call to the Johnson's that left Marty baffled and curious.

On the way over to Marty's house, Anne tuned the car radio to the local station. It was almost 11 a.m. so there was bound to be a break for news headlines. "Does anyone else in the world know about this?" Anne asked her radio.

The radio station broke for news, "This is WGRC 1340 with the top headlines. I'm Barry Martin. The president is visiting Beirut today in the ongoing effort to rebuild Lebanon—What? Wait, folks. This is just coming in . . . a small portion of the Jewish and Christian Bibles has reappeared in print. The scholars we interviewed said that it is a portion of the book written by the prophet Jeremiah. It is known as the text Jeremiah 31:31–34 in which God promises to make a new covenant with his people. While there is much shock and jubilation about this small portion of the Bible reappearing, scholars are now wondering why this particular text of Scripture has appeared, and they are wondering if more portions may appear. We'll keep you updated with this breaking story.

"In other news, the president has promised, working with allies, to help in the restoration of war-torn Lebanon . . ."

Anne pulled into Marty's driveway, noting that Nancy had already arrived. The garage door was open so Anne ran to the kitchen door inside the back of the garage. As she neared it, the door opened and Marty and Nancy grabbed her and pulled her in.

"Can you believe this?" Marty said.

"Not hardly," said Anne, "but I just heard about it on the news."

"We heard, too," Nancy said gleefully.

Anne and Nancy sat down at the kitchen table and opened their Bibles to the place they had bookmarked. Marty returned to the table with her Bible.

"Where is it?" she asked.

Anne replied, "Jeremiah 31, near the middle of the Bible. Open it near the middle and follow the chapter headings. That's what I did."

Marty began to do as instructed. To her amazement she, too, saw words on her formerly blank pages. She began to read, slowly and aloud.

> *"For I will take you out of the nations; I will gather you from all the countries and bring you back into your own land. I will sprinkle clean water on you, and you will be clean; I will cleanse you from all your impurities and from all your idols. I will give you a new heart and put a new spirit in you; I will remove from you your heart of stone and give you a heart of flesh. And I will put my Spirit in you and move you to follow my decrees and be careful to keep my laws. You will live in the land I gave your forefathers; you will be my people, and I will be your God."*

"Amazing," Marty said.

Anne and Nancy looked confused.

"Marty, that's not what's in our Bibles," Nancy said.

"What?"

"We've got different words than the ones you just read." Anne joined in. "Yours are a little similar, but different. Read them, again, Marty."

Marty did.

Anne then read the words in her Bible.

Nancy said, "What I have matches what Anne read."

"What is this?" Marty was puzzled. "I . . . I've paged past Jeremiah. I'm not in Jeremiah at all. I think I've got words *from Ezekiel*! It's his record of the promise of the new covenant. I've got words from another author, from another book. Do you know what this means?"

Anne and Nancy looked blank.

"More of the Bible has reappeared since you called me!"

Marty slowly turned back some more pages in her Bible and found another page of text. "Here's your Jeremiah passage!" she said hurriedly. "Turn a few pages ahead, you guys, in your Bibles! Quick!"

Anne and Nancy did so, coming to the Ezekiel text that Marty read.

The three women sat stunned. Two texts from two different books were in their Bibles. They wondered to themselves how fast this would be known and celebrated around the world.

Marty's phone rang.

"I know, I know, Harry," Marty said, laughing. "Anne, Nancy, and I just read them."

The *ABC World News Tonight* program led with the story of the reappearing Old Testament texts.

● ● ●

FEBRUARY 22

Ben Cook was one of many who got up in the morning and searched the Bible to see if any more Scriptures had appeared besides the texts from Jeremiah and Ezekiel. After getting his morning paper and making his fresh ground bean coffee, he would turn to where the Gospel of John should be. Each morning those pages were blank. Each morning he was disappointed. Nothing against old Jeremiah and Ezekiel, but he longed for John's Gospel to return . . . if it ever would. For some reason, perhaps because of John 3:16, John's Gospel was the favorite Gospel of many people. Often new converts were encouraged to read John's Gospel. Ben remembered reading it when he was converted to Jesus while in college. He missed it.

The news on TV, in the papers, in magazines carried many stories about the reappearance of the two Old Testament texts now in print. The words could be written and recorded and they remained. Ancient manuscripts of the Old Testament contained those two texts as if they had never disappeared.

In a recent home group meeting at the Roberts' house, there had been a lot of excitement about the Bible being in print again, even if it was such a little set of verses. Dr. Johnson had reported that Jewish and Christian scholars were fascinated by this return of a portion of the Old Testament and that there was much speculation as to why these specific texts had appeared.

"You have no doubt noted the similarity in words and theme that Jeremiah and Ezekiel wrote." Harold Johnson had addressed the excited group. "These are words of promise from God to write or place his words by his Spirit into human hearts. This promise is known as the New Covenant. Instead of God's Word written in stone—like the commandments of Moses—God would do some sort of internal work in human lives. People would know God, love God, and obey his will and words and ways. These texts that have reappeared describe an absolute overhaul in how God would relate to human beings—making his ways and will known. I don't think these twin texts have ever received so much attention!"

○ ○ ○

MARCH 2
Ben took a sip of coffee, then picked up his Bible and randomly thumbed through it. He came across the Jeremiah and Ezekiel texts and took time to read them. He came to the notes (still in print in his Bible) explaining the four hundred silent years between the Old and New Testaments. The white pages beyond he knew to be the New Testament. He rummaged on slowly, not really paying attention since he knew them all to be blank. His mind pondered the promises of the New Covenant. God promised to put his very own Spirit in people—the Holy Spirit. The way the New Covenant life could truly be lived was by the presence and power of the Spirit of God. But then a word caught his eyes—"dwelling." *Dwelling?* And it was among a few other words in the middle of a page. He stopped his mindless page turning and carefully paged back. There they were, clear and neat:

> The Word became flesh and made his dwelling among us. We have seen his glory, the glory of the One and Only, who came from the Father, full of grace and truth.

Ben dropped his Bible and swung out his arms like he was going to hug Anne after not seeing her for a long time. This happened instantly, so quickly that he had knocked over his coffee cup. Coffee splattered everywhere. Ben didn't care. He shouted excitedly, "John 1:14! I learned this verse in college. It's about Jesus, the Word of God, becoming a human being and 'dwelling' with us! This is about the incarnation of God!"

Ben called out for Anne as he grabbed his phone to call Steve Roberts, "Anne, get your Bible! Quick! John's back!"

"Hello, this is Steve."

"Steve! Pastor Steve! John 1:14 is in my Bible . . . in print!"

"I know, isn't it great!" Steve laughed. "It's in my Bible, too. I called Dr. Johnson this morning when I saw it. He said it was in both his English and his Greek New Testaments. The news stations are being contacted about it right now. Hey, turn a few pages forward. Do you see anything else?"

Ben again paged slowly forward until he came to these words at the top of a left page:

"You diligently study the Scriptures because you think that by them you possess eternal life. These are the Scriptures that testify about me, yet you refuse to come to me to have life."

"Steve, I just read the words. This is great! First John 1:14 and now John 5:39–40, too!"

"I know, isn't it great! We have parts of the New Testament, the Gospel of John back in print. Fantastic!"

"Man, Steve, I wonder what the scholars will tell us about the significance of these two texts reappearing? Did Dr. Johnson say anything?"

"He said it was too early to say, but he definitely feels that these verses are somehow linked to the two texts from the Old Testament, to the words of Jeremiah and Ezekiel about the New Covenant. Intriguing, isn't it?"

"You bet it is! 'The Word became flesh and made his dwelling among us.' I'm no scholar, but I can see how God putting his Word in our hearts by the Spirit is like 'the Word becoming flesh.' Am I thinking right about that, Steve?"

"I think so. Dr. Johnson made that same comparison. He said that he thinks that the John 1:14 passage may be some sort of key to the puzzle of the returning verses. You're more of a scholar than you know, Ben," Steve chuckled.

Ben was both embarrassed and flattered. *Me, a Bible scholar? No way.*

"Hey, Ben, I gotta go. I've got a meeting with some other pastors in about twenty minutes. Thanks for calling. We'll keep in touch."

"Sure, Steve. See you soon. Thanks for talking. Bye."

Ben hung up and grinned. The Gospel of John, his favorite was back. Sure, not totally, but enough to make him feel really good inside. *And I am a budding scholar, too. Right on.*

That night Carl Wilson led off *ABC World News Tonight* with the story about parts of the Gospel of John reappearing on the pages of New Testaments around the world.

◌ ◌ ◌

MARCH 23—EASTER SUNDAY
Karla Myers did not like to waste anything. She was a collector, a hoarder, a saver, a coupon clipper. She could do things with a box of rice that was fit for a king. Being a missionary you learn to be frugal.

So Karla was considering using the blank pages of her Bible as a journal. Instead of tossing it aside, she would daily use the blank pages to record her prayers, her dreams and her personal challenges. She would also keep track of travel details, family issues, missionary ministry, and personal growth as a Christian. What better place to write than on blank pages in a Bible? *But what if words return on the pages I write on?* she wondered. *What if I had written on the pages of Jeremiah 31? Maybe being so frugal in this instance isn't such a good idea.*

She liked to get up at 6:00 a.m. and to read and journal. She enjoyed the devotional writings of Oswald Chambers, A.W. Tozer, and Henri Nouwen. She had recently been introduced by Tracy to two books by a young writer named Donald Miller—*Blue Like Jazz* and *Through Painted Deserts*. Karla liked to read, and if Tracy liked a book, Karla knew that she would like it too. She had started reading *Blue Like Jazz* and hadn't been able to put it down. He certainly wasn't a writer like Oswald Chambers, but she detected a fire in Donald Miller similar to that in Oswald Chambers.

She felt excited today because it was Easter Sunday. *The greatest surprise on the planet happened today,* she thought. Yet her excitement was tinged with sadness. *What will Easter be like this year . . . without the Bible?* She opened her blank Bible to do some reflecting on some of Donald Miller's thoughts. She had small, plastic paper clips in Jeremiah, Ezekiel, and John to remind her where the words of the Bible had reappeared. She was journaling on pages at the beginning of the Bible. *Sorry, Moses,* she mused.

As she reached for a pen, she accidentally knocked her Bible off the edge of the small writing desk in the guest bedroom—the room that the DeLanos were letting them use during their furlough in Grand Rivers. As she reached for her Bible, she noticed some words on the page it had fallen open to. She also noticed that the page was not marked with a paper clip. *Could it be that another part of the Bible had come back in print?* She carefully picked up her Bible keeping the words in sight.

With the Bible open flat on the desk, Karla read:

> *You yourselves are our letter, written on our hearts, known and read by everybody. You show that you are a letter from Christ, the result of our ministry, written not with ink but with the Spirit of the living God, not on tablets of stone but on tablets of human hearts.*

"Why this is 2 Corinthians," Karla said aloud, glancing up at the book name printed at the top corner of the page. "This is not Jeremiah or Ezekiel or John. These are words from Paul the Apostle! I'm reading a portion of a New Testament letter. Oh Lord, what are you doing to us? This is wonderful! I just knew you had a surprise for me, Lord."

Karla quietly got up and walked over to the side of the bed where Hank was still sleeping. "Hank, Hank, wake up. Wake up, dear," she said.

Hank snorted and rolled over and opened his eyes.

He said, "Yeah, Karla, what is it? What time is it?"

"Hank, it's Easter Sunday. Guess what? Part of 2 Corinthians is in print in my Bible. There is a portion of Paul's letter clear as day. Oh it's all just so wonderful!"

Hank, now fully awake, sat up and looked at the page that Karla was excitedly pointing to. There they were, *You yourselves are our letter, written on our hearts, known and read by everybody. You show that you are a letter from Christ, the result of our ministry, written not with ink but with the Spirit of the living God, not on tablets of stone but on tablets of human hearts.*

"Karla, this is amazing. The Bible is reappearing piecemeal. I don't understand why, but I sure am glad. Does anyone else know?"

"I just now found it and you're the first one I've told."

"Are the DeLanos up?"

"I think so. I think I heard Nancy making breakfast."

"Let's go show her and Jim."

◦ ◦ ◦

Across town, Harold Johnson was already up and studying John 1:14 and 5:39–40, comparing those verses with the Jeremiah and Ezekiel texts. That it was Easter Sunday had not yet dawned on him. He stopped and closed his eyes. *Why are only these verses reappearing . . . of all the verses in the Bible . . . why these?* He decided to read the texts from beginning to end in the order they had reappeared.

> *"The time is coming," declares the* Lord,
> *"when I will make a new covenant*
> *with the house of Israel*
> *and with the house of Judah.*
> *It will not be like the covenant*
> *I made with their forefathers*
> *when I took them by the hand*
> *to lead them out of Egypt,*
> *because they broke my covenant,*
> *though I was a husband to them,"*
> *declares the Lord.*

> "This is the covenant I will make with the house of Israel
>   after that time," declares the Lord.
>   "I will put my law in their minds
>   and write it on their hearts.
>   I will be their God,
>   and they will be my people.
> "No longer will a man teach his neighbor,
>   or a man his brother, saying, 'Know the Lord,'
>   because they will all know me,
>   from the least of them to the greatest,"
>   declares the Lord.
>   "For I will forgive their wickedness
>   and will remember their sins no more."

> "For I will take you out of the nations; I will gather you from all the countries and bring you back into your own land. I will sprinkle clean water on you, and you will be clean; I will cleanse you from all your impurities and from all your idols. I will give you a new heart and put a new spirit in you; I will remove from you your heart of stone and give you a heart of flesh. And I will put my Spirit in you and move you to follow my decrees and be careful to keep my laws. You will live in the land I gave your forefathers; you will be my people, and I will be your God."

> "The Word became flesh and made his dwelling among us. We have seen his glory, the glory of the One and Only, who came from the Father, full of grace and truth."

> "You diligently study the Scriptures because you think that by them you possess eternal life. These are the Scriptures that testify about me, yet you refuse to come to me to have life."

When Harold was finished, he began jotting down words and phrases that stood out from what he had read.

> *God says "I will" . . . "I will" over and over . . . "in their minds" . . . "on their hearts" . . . a new heart . . . heart of stone . . . heart of flesh . . . new spirit . . . put my Spirit . . . in you . . . in you . . . the Word became flesh . . .*

He underlined "<u>flesh</u>" in the John 1 passage, then flipped back to Ezekiel and underlined it there too.

. . . you diligently study the Scriptures . . . yet <u>refuse</u> to come to <u>me</u>. Underlining the words "refuse" and "me" in John 5:40, Harold tapped his pen against his chin and leaned back in his chair. *What can this mean?*

He was pulled out of his deep pondering by the sound of the phone ringing.

"Hello, this is Harold Johnson."

"Happy Easter, Harold! This is Hank Myers. Guess what? Karla was getting ready to journal on the blank pages of her Bible this morning and discovered that 2 Corinthians 3:2–3 were back in print. We showed the verses to the DeLanos and the verses are in their Bibles, too."

"What verses did you say?" Harold reached for his Bible, his heart racing.

"Second Corinthians 3:2–3. I'll read them to you."

You yourselves are our letter, written on our hearts, known and read by everybody. You show that you are a letter from Christ, the result of our ministry, written not with ink but with the Spirit of the living God, not on tablets of stone but on tablets of human hearts.

"Unbelievable," Harold muttered slowly in awe, more to himself than to Hank.

"What's that, Harold? What did you say?" Hank asked.

Silence.

"Harold, are you there?"

"Hmm? Oh yes, sorry Hank, I was just thinking . . ." Harold trailed off. "What did you say a moment ago?"

"I don't know what you mean? I just said, 'Happy Easter,' and that Karla had found the 2 Corinthians 3 text."

"*Easter.* It's Easter today and these particular verses from Paul reappear. Hmmm, that's got to be part of the, the pattern. This can't be just a random reappearance. I think that there is a definite shape here or some unified theme to all these verses that are coming back into print. The ruling consensus seems to be that the texts promising a new covenant need more attention than they've recently received in biblical and theological studies. Now, because of the events of their remarkable reappearance, the attention of the whole biblical world is intently focused on these few scriptural words.

"Many scholars, Christians in particular, admit that there was a dumbing down about this dramatic change promised by God. The radical change initiated by Jesus was the new way God would relate to human beings. This got lost. The New Covenant differs greatly from the Old Covenant. Some Christians don't even know the difference between the Old Testament and New Testament. Things got terribly blurred. Many people are either ignorant of or simply misunderstand the startling new ways God relates to his people.

"What are those startling new ways, Harold?" Hank asked.

"That's the question, Hank. The current biblical and theological task is to determine those differences, but an obvious one, for sure, is that God intends for his words to be in human beings and work out from human beings into the world. From tablets of stone to the fleshiness of human hearts as the two texts present—from external to internal."

"What does all this mean, Harold? I mean, in a nut shell? "

"I don't want to jump to conclusions, but I think it's about God's desire, even will, that his Word become incarnate in people. Just as Jesus is alive, I think God wants his Word to be alive in us. Certainly John 1:14 is a key passage that emphasizes that point with the incarnation of Jesus—'the Word became flesh.' It may be too early to say for sure. I'll call a meeting of the Committee of Concern and find out what they think and what they are hearing from others."

"Well, we just wanted to let you know the good news. I'll let you get back to—Uh, hang on a minute, would you, Harold?"

Harold heard Hank set the phone down, and could faintly hear his muffled voice talking excitedly to Karla. Before long, Hank was back on the line.

"Harold, are you there? You're not going to believe this! Karla says that a part of 2 Corinthians 5 has reappeared, too. Let me read it."

And he died for all, that those who live should no longer live for themselves but for him who died for them and was raised again.

So from now on we regard no one from a worldly point of view. Though we once regarded Christ in this way, we do so no longer. Therefore, if anyone is in Christ, he is a new creation; the old has gone, the new has come! All this is from God, who reconciled us to himself through Christ and gave us the ministry of reconciliation: that God was reconciling the world to himself in Christ, not counting men's sins against them. And he has committed to us the message of reconciliation.

"Unbelievable," Harold muttered again.
"This *is* unbelievable, isn't it, Harold?"
"Just incredible," Harold whispered. "Easter Sunday. Unbelievable."

◦ ◦ ◦

APRIL 27
"Did anyone see *ABC's World News Tonight* last evening with Carl Wilson?" Dr. Katherine Westbrook asked those gathered around the conference table. The Committee of Concern for the Great Lakes region had been convened at the request of Harold Johnson.

"I saw it," responded Father Demitri Kassius of the Greek Orthodox Church, "and it was amazing to see a major news anchor actually glad that the Bible was returning. He seemed thankful that parts of the Scripture were reappearing."

"Who would have thought the Bible would be the news story of the year?" marveled Father James Pulaski, the Catholic priest.

Katherine brought the meeting to order. "Friends, Harry has called this meeting because he wants to discuss the sequence and content of the reappearing Scriptures. I admit that I, too, have been fascinated to see a pattern, and I'm sure you have noted it too."

"It's undeniable," admitted Rabbi Spielman, "even though I cannot comment on it as much as all of you can. I'm intrigued by the New Testament passages, but cannot delve into their implications."

"There is a pattern or theme," Harold affirmed. "A pattern that is conceptually linked, even semantically cohesive." Harold paused, and then spoke the next words firmly, almost staccato, for emphasis. "*I am convinced it is about God's desire to have the written Word come alive and expressed in and through human beings.* The reappearance of John 1:14 '. . . the Word became flesh . . .' was the key for me. Because John 1:14 emphasizes the Word becoming flesh, I felt something crucial was being stressed. What do the rest of you think?"

Katherine was the first to respond. "Well, Harry, as a scholar of oral history and transmission, I have been fascinated with the way people of faith have awakened to the power and beauty of the Bible *heard*. Oral transmission creates a unique and different set of dynamics than reading does, or seeing words in print. When we read the Word we are in charge; sight makes us the center of attention. But when we *hear* the Word, we are recipients and we feel an instinct to respond. The Hebrew language bears this out—the word for 'listen' is the same as the word for 'obey.' Hearing the Word draws out our truly human qualities. We are relational, communal beings. I can read in isolation, but when I am addressed verbally, orally, I am immediately located in relational, or interpersonal space. I emphasize: Hearing the Word takes us out of the position of 'being in charge' of the word . . . or words. I don't think Jesus was just being cute by repeatedly saying, 'Let the one who has ears to hear, hear.' He did not say, 'Let the one who has eyes, see.' Hearing, that is, listening with the will, is an incredible stewardship. In hearing, we are receiving. We are in the humbled position. I repeat: When we hear, we are not in charge."

"I think that the reports we are receiving about a global interest in the Bible and many choosing to follow Jesus and his Way, with all due respect Rabbi Spielman . . ."

"No need to apologize, I understand what you're saying, Katherine," the Rabbi said.

Katherine continued, "What I was going to say was 'the Way of Jesus' seems to be the emphasis of these reappearing texts. Jesus of Nazareth is taking the preeminent place. That may be hard for Rabbi Spielman and many other of our Jewish friends to accept."

"What I'm hearing," said Father Demitri, "is a profound cooperation in Eastern and Western Europe among various Orthodox, Catholic, Jewish, and Protestant groups, scholars, and spiritual leaders, to keep the Word of God alive in speech. Not only that, but they are also gathering to engage one another in how to best guide, comfort, and encourage the faithful in their regions. The cooperation is amazing."

"We've seen that here in the States, too, among the various theological and denominational factions," said Harold. "And it's not as if differences are ignored; they're just placed in a much lower place on the priority scale. So, what do you think is the meaning of the pattern?"

"I thought I saw a pattern, but I can't factor in the John 5:39–40 text," said Father James. "Why the play of 'studying the Scriptures diligently' against 'refusing to come to Jesus'?"

"Any thoughts on that question? Anyone?" Harold asked.

"Let's look at that text and hear it," suggested Katherine.

The sound of rustling pages filled the quiet conference room as the Committee searched for John 5:39–40 in their mostly blank Bibles.

"Oh, my God! Excuse my excitement, but look at this! I've found part of Jesus' prayer in John 17," Father James shouted.

"What!" the rest of the Committee said in surprised unison.

"I've found it, too," Katherine said. "Here, I'll read it."

> *"I have given them the glory that you gave me, that they may be one as we are one: I in them and you in me. May they be brought to complete unity to let the world know that you sent me and have loved them even as you have loved me."*

"Unbelievable," muttered Harold Johnson as he gazed at John 17:22–23 in his Greek New Testament. "It's really there . . . the pattern."

"What, Harry? What did you say?" asked Rabbi Spielman.

"I am convinced even more with this John 17 text that it is undeniable that we are receiving an emphatic message about the purposes of the Bible in human lives. It scares me to think that God may have been behind the disappearance of his word and is now dramatically trying to tell us something by these reappearing texts . . . beginning with the promise of a 'new covenant.' Now, hear me, I'm not certain that God is behind all this; I'm not saying that God is the cause of the Bible going out of print, but perhaps God has his hand in the reappearance of these verses. I don't know. They can't just randomly, willy-nilly be coming back into print."

What do you think is God's message, Harry?" asked Katherine.

Harold answered, "I'm sorry for repeating myself. I sometimes feel like I am just thinking out loud. I admit that I appear to have become somewhat obsessed with all this."

Harold paused and gathered his thoughts. He spoke more deliberately.

"I think it's a pattern emphasizing that God wants his Word fleshed out . . . not just ink on paper or commands chiseled in stone. These verses are about one thing: God's Word as a living, seeing, touching, talking, caring, warning, inviting reality; a reality *in flesh and blood*. First in his people *Israel*, then preeminently in *Jesus the Christ* and now in his *Church*—the 'body of Christ' in all its various expressions around the world—'You yourselves are our letter, written on our hearts, known and read by everybody.' God is writing his Word with invisible ink—the presence of the Holy Spirit of God. Paul continues in 2 Corinthians 3, 'You show that *you are a letter from Christ*, the result of our ministry, written *not with ink* but *with the Spirit of the living God*, not on tablets of stone but on tablets of *human hearts*.' God wants a people—living in unity and love, a unity and love that reflect the very life of the Trinitarian God—a people that Jesus himself prayed for and asked his Father for, as we see here in this newest text to appear on the scene."

Harold stopped and let out a deep sigh. He was convinced that he was understanding these things correctly. He also was becoming more settled that God surely was the One behind all the reappearance of the verses.

"I agree with the message of these reappearing texts, Harold," Father James said, "but the Vatican is still going along the line that Satan, the adversary, thief, and liar, is behind the absence of the Bible. The leading Catholic scholars are proposing that Satan somehow stole the Bible, and Jesus, *Christus Victor*, is winning it back. They contend that there is some hidden, cosmic battle being waged as we meet right now. It's what the Holy Father is declaring to the global Catholic Church."

"And I can't say the Pope is wrong on that, Jim, but I can't say he's correct either," Harold replied. "It's all just speculation really as to the cause of the *disappearance* of the Bible. That did seem so random and frightening. But these verses are reappearing in a way that shows there is *an intelligence* behind them with a specific message to communicate. Don't you think?"

"It would certainly seem that way," Jim responded.

"Perhaps," Father Demitri said, "we should not focus so much on *cause*, but focus instead on *response* and *results*. The creation of MMS's and the Bible Listening Rooms was unforeseen; the global cooperation of the Church is a phenomenon many have prayed about, but never actually thought would get to the level that we are experiencing and hearing reported. It seems to me that the basic message of the reappearing verses is: 'It's about time. You're finally getting it right.' Like Katherine has said, people are hearing the words of God and are responding. I saw an interview on TV last night where a reporter was asking young people coming out of a Bible Listening Room in Paris what they thought. One of them responded, 'We never knew of a Jesus who was such a brave and caring person. His love for the little guy, the poor, and the marginalized was new to us. His bravery in the face of injustice was compelling. We used to think Jesus was a bore who reigned over a dead, depressing church. All dressed up and meaningless.' These young people had listened to the Gospel of Luke."

"You know, Demitri, I've heard similar interviews with young people in Germany, New Zealand, the Philippines, and Ethiopia," Katherine pointed out.

"I have also heard that in closed Muslim countries, the Bible's Story is spreading like wildfire among young people," Rabbi Spielman added.

"And I don't know about you," Father Demitri eagerly continued, "but I don't think all this attention and positive reaction is just because the Bible has been memorized. It is because the Bible's Story is finally being heard as it was originally given. The Bible is not 'my book' or 'your book.' It was given to communities, through communities, for communities. The Bible is a book for the whole world. It was given to unite, not divide the church. I think this whole situation with the Bible disappearing has been to teach us a valuable lesson—even if it was in a very painful, and at first, frightening way."

"Thanks, Demitri, for urging us to look at the results of and responses to this whole situation rather than endlessly rummaging around for the cause. And thanks to all of you for gathering to hear me out and share your insights," said Harold Johnson. "I'm glad to hear that I'm not making stuff up or heading in a wrong direction."

"But what about the John 5:39-40 text?" Katherine asked.

"Oh, yeah, that text," said Harold, "reminds us how easily we can get absorbed in a book, even a holy one, and neglect or even resist the One the Bible is about. The Bible can be studied very diligently, but if that study does not lead us to Messiah, to Jesus, we miss the whole point of the Bible's Story. God is a person revealed exactly in the person of Jesus. The Bible rightly read leads us to him. This kind of goes along with what you were saying earlier, Katherine. With all due respect, Rabbi Spielman."

"Again, I understand," replied the Rabbi softly.

The Committee of Concern closed with a word of prayer and then dismissed. Later that evening each of the members of the committee watched, as did millions of other viewers worldwide, as the major television networks reported astounding news: *all* the content of the books of Jeremiah and Ezekiel had reappeared, as had *all* of the Gospel of John, the *entire* books of 1 and 2 Corinthians, *all* one hundred and fifty Psalms, and the *complete* book of Ephesians. The Bible was making a comeback.

○ ○ ○

MAY 1

The small group meeting at Steve and Betsy Roberts' house was buzzing with excitement. The Myers had heard from Seigi in Nabire that all their translation work on the Gospel of John had reappeared simultaneously with the reappearance of the Gospel of John around the world. Hank and Karla were thrilled and could make plans to return to the Vahudati people after three more days of rest.

"We're going back to be with the people we love and serve," Hank said.

"Not that we don't love all of you!" Karla added. "Because we do. You've been such a help to us during this time, especially to Hank."

Hank agreed, saying, "I came home so depressed, even angry. I felt wasted and used. I couldn't keep from asking why all our work simply vanished. Over these past months I've learned that God wants me to be a living 'translation' of his Word even as I work hard to get his Word into the Vahudati language. You all have been God's living Word to Karla and me. Thank you so much."

Steve Roberts was thrilled by the growth of TRCC as all kinds of people came there: wondering about God, frightened by the loss of the Bible, curious about what was going on in the world. Many of them stuck around. Now that things were stabilizing, he and Betsy were going to take a short break, a brief sabbatical trip to recover from the emotional, spiritual, and physical strain the months with no Bible had on them.

"What are you guys going to do on sabbatical?" asked Nancy DeLano.

"Well, I for one am going to savor each word of the Psalms," replied Betsy.

"I'm going to savor Betsy," laughed Steve. Betsy blushed red.

"Get a room!" said Luci laughing.

"Oh, we will!" laughed Steve.

The Johnsons were thrilled that Harold was back teaching his exegesis of the Greek New Testament Gospel of John. He was glad to write εν αρχη ην ο λογοσ on the black board and see it stay there.

"I still can't believe I asked the students about disappearing chalk. Those bewildered young people must have thought I was a nutcase," he laughed.

"Harold, you are a nutcase, but a lovable one," Steve teased. "But in all seriousness, thanks so much for helping us with a lot of questions and being honest when you didn't know the answers. Thanks, too, for giving your time to be on the Committee of Concern. We learned a lot from you as you reported on the meetings."

Nancy DeLano spoke up. "I'm starting back up my after-school Bible club next week. I'm so glad; and I've heard the kids are eager to start. I hope I never see the words of Scripture disappear again, but if I do, I'll know it's not the end of the world." Jim squeezed her hand.

"Hear, hear! I second that emotion," said Luci. "When the Bible vanished, God showed up all the more through all of you. Like Dr. Johnson reminded us from 2 Corinthians 3:2–3: you, my small group, are Christ's letter to me and when I 'read' you, I discovered love and care and forgiveness and, most of all, hope. I'm still holding out hope for Wayne."

"I am too, Luci," Tracy said. "I have loved watching you become a follower of Jesus and begin to make good decisions as a Christian woman. It has been so reassuring to me that the good news of God's great love still deeply changes people's lives. All this happened with no Bible around. It happened because, as you said, we were the Bible to you. I think that is fantastic. The way that it's supposed to be. I'm praying God will send people into Wayne's life that will be the Bible to him."

Ben looked at Anne, and took her hand. "I feel a lot like you, Tracy. I have been so blessed by watching Anne in her involvement with the mission memory seminar, helping people hear the Psalms. It made me aware of how precious the *whole* Story of God's love is as it comes to us through Moses, and David, and the prophets, and Jesus, and the Church. I've heard that some treat the Bible like it's a textbook or handbook or rulebook. But the Bible is so much more than a book of religious content. It's a grand Story of God's great love for this planet."

"I agree, Ben," Harold said. "It's not about the fact that so many people have memorized the Word of God; they have let it get down *into their hearts*, not just their heads. They let it shape their vision of the world, their values for life choices, their love and forgiveness for those who grieve or hurt them. And so much more."

Ben agreed, "You know, it seems that we viewed the Bible like the Israelites viewed the Old Covenant chiseled in stone, only we had it printed on paper. It was 'out there' commanding us, watching us, judging us, rather than being 'in here'"—he tapped his heart—"shaping, transforming, I mean, *deeply* changing us."

Anne spoke softly and confidently:

> *The* Lord *is my light and my salvation—*
> *whom shall I fear?*
> *The* Lord *is the stronghold of my life—*
> *of whom shall I be afraid?*
> *When evil men advance against me*
> *to devour my flesh,*
> *when my enemies and my foes attack me,*
> *they will stumble and fall.*
> *Though an army besiege me,*
> *my heart will not fear;*
> *though war break out against me,*
> *even then will I be confident.*
> *One thing I ask of the* Lord,
> *this is what I seek:*
> *that I may dwell in the house of the* Lord
> *all the days of my life,*
> *to gaze upon the beauty of the* Lord
> *and to seek him in his temple.*
> *For in the day of trouble*
> *he will keep me safe in his dwelling;*
> *he will hide me in the shelter of his tabernacle*
> *and set me high upon a rock.*
> *Then my head will be exalted*
> *above the enemies who surround me;*
> *at his tabernacle will I sacrifice with shouts of joy;*
> *I will sing and make music to the* Lord.
> *Hear my voice when I call, O* Lord;
> *be merciful to me and answer me.*
> *My heart says of you, "Seek his face!"*
> *Your face,* Lord, *I will seek.*
> *Do not hide your face from me,*
> *do not turn your servant away in anger;*

> *you have been my helper.*
> *Do not reject me or forsake me,*
> *O God my Savior.*
> *Though my father and mother forsake me,*
> *the* L*ORD* *will receive me.*
> *Teach me your way, O* L*ORD*;
> *lead me in a straight path*
> *because of my oppressors.*
> *Do not turn me over to the desire of my foes,*
> *for false witnesses rise up against me,*
> *breathing out violence.*
> *I am still confident of this:*
> *I will see the goodness of the* L*ORD*
> *in the land of the living.*
> *Wait for the* L*ORD*;
> *be strong and take heart*
> *and wait for the* L*ORD*.

The group was quiet, and tears flowed from the eyes of all.

Harold spoke softly, "You know, as important as it is to memorize Scripture and as powerful as it is to hear it, I think we should all keep sight of the most important lesson from this whole chaotic string of events, the message from the first reappearing texts: *God wants his Word made flesh.* He wants it spoken and lived, proclaimed and performed. The Bible is like a grand play about God's embracing grace, and God is looking for people to audition for the parts. I think N. T. Wright used that metaphor once. The young Corinthian church was able to be 'a letter of Christ read by everyone' without having memorized a thing, as far as we know. They just surrendered to Jesus, received his salvation, and started living it out. Not perfectly we know, but they were recipients of the New Covenant and so the Holy Spirit was in them, writing God's words on their hearts. And those words looked just like Jesus. What an unbelievable reality."

Steve sighed happily. "Well, we've had a great time this evening, but it's getting late. I'd like to tell you a story I heard and then I'd like for us to gather around Hank and Karla and pray for the few days they have left with us and for their continuing work in Irian Jaya.

"The story is from a tradition of the church, and I'm not sure which one—Greek Orthodox, Russian Orthodox, Catholic—I don't know, but it is based on the fact that on Good Friday when Jesus died, they wrapped him in cloths and buried him. The tradition goes like this: Every year, on Good Friday, the cross in the church is covered and the leaders dramatize putting Jesus' corpse in a well, the symbol of a tomb. But it doesn't stop there. The leaders also close the Bible, remove it from its sacred stand, wrap it in cloth, and place it in the 'tomb' as well. Then on Easter, both Jesus and the Bible are celebrated as rising from the dead! The powerful message proclaimed through these actions is this: without the living Christ the Bible has no message for us. Remember the risen, yet unrecognized, Jesus walking with his two dejected disciples on the road to Emmaus? He opened the Scriptures—the risen Christ gave them understanding—and later they said to one another, 'Were not our hearts burning within us while he opened the Scriptures to us?'

"Over the past several months, we have experienced something similar in some ways. The Bible was buried, so to speak; it disappeared from us. The difference for us was that the living Christ was not buried. He is still alive forever. When the Bible 'died,' God was more alive than ever!"

"Amen!" shouted Nancy DeLano.

"Well said, Steve," agreed Harold Johnson.

"Our God reigns!" echoed Tracy and Luci.

"Now, let's pray for the Myers. And while we're praying, let's pray for Wayne, too. And let's pray that God's Word will fall like rain all around the world and produce crops of a hundred fold."

○ ○ ○

Wayne Unger stretched out on the bed, watching a rerun of *Alias* on TV in his hotel room. His company had sent him on an errand to a warehouse in North Chicago to pick up some specialized flooring tiles for a project in Grand Rivers. He had been caught in freeway, rush-hour traffic near the O'Hare airport and had gotten to the North

Chicago company just in time to load up his truck before they closed. He had found a room at a cheap hotel to spend the night, a decision endorsed by his boss when he called in about the unexpected traffic. He had ordered a pizza, bought a six-pack of beer at the nearby convenience store, and settled down in front of the TV in his hotel room.

He found himself missing Luci. Sure, he was taking care of himself. Yet he had to admit that he was lonely. He didn't like eating alone, sleeping alone, doing life alone. But there was no way he was going to go to Three Rivers Church. He felt that Luci's religious demands were unfair and, even more importantly, idealistic. And Wayne defined himself as a realist. He was a self-guided man who liked being the captain of his soul.

"Oh, Luci, why did you have to get religion?" he heard himself say.

Gee, get a hold on yourself, buddy. So Luci left you. Get a grip! You can make it. Look, you've made it this far.

Suddenly the *Alias* program was broken into with a breaking news report. An excited Carl Wilson of *ABC News* reported that the Vatican was reporting that the entire Bible was back in print and in all the other medium that it had disappeared from. A Vatican official read a brief message from the Pope celebrating the return of the precious gift of the Holy Scriptures. Then, the face of Reverend Jimmy Blake was on the screen being personally interviewed by Wilson.

"Reverend Blake, what do you think of this amazing event—the reappearance of the Bible in print and all other forms of recording?"

"Well, Mr. Wilson, I first just want to thank God that the Scriptures are in the hands of God's people again. It is not out of print any longer. The Holy Bible tells us of God's great love through his Son Jesus Christ who died on the cross for the sins of this world. I am so glad. And my father, Truman, rejoices as well."

"Reverend Blake, do you or your father or any other religious leaders have any idea as to *the cause* of the disappearance of the Bible?"

"Well, Carl, why the Bible disappeared has been the big question, but from all that I'm hearing, no one can prove who did this shocking thing or why. As you probably have heard, some think God did it to teach us all a lesson, and others, bless their hearts, think the Devil did it. Who knows? I don't pretend to know. All I know is that the Bible is back. People for months were simply hearing the Bible, and so many, especially young people, are spreading around this planet with the good news of God's great love, serving the poor, caring for the sick, and speaking for the oppressed. Humanitarian agencies and missions groups have all expanded greatly over the past months. It's truly amazing. It's a miracle."

"Thank you, Reverend."

Carl Wilson repeated the breaking headline: the entire Bible had reappeared. "Stay tuned for breaking developments in this story. Good night."

"Good night to you," Wayne said, clicking off the TV. After a moment, he rolled over to the nightstand next to the bed. He opened the drawer and saw it there, just as he expected: a Gideon's Bible. He pulled it out and opened to the first pages. Flipping past the table of contents, he saw the opening verse of the Bible: "In the beginning God created the heavens and the earth." He thumbed through the rest of the pages. It was all there, right to the end:

> *He who testifies to these things says, "Yes, I am coming soon."*
> *Amen. Come, Lord Jesus.*
> *The grace of the Lord Jesus be with God's people. Amen.*

Wayne closed the Bible and put it back in the drawer.

Epilogue

JUNE 20

A special report from Manchester, England, reported the happy return of the ancient Greek script on P52—the John Rylands papyrus. Many other ancient biblical manuscripts, written in Greek, Latin, Syriac, Coptic, and other languages, which had also lost their lettering, were all back in fine shape as though nothing had happened.

While that report was being watched by Ben and Anne Cook in their River Valley home, the Reverend Randy Joe Jason was finishing his day in the rough country of Mozambique, Africa.

Brother Randy Joe and his family lived as missionaries in the far—and often dangerous—reaches of this poor African country. The kinds of work they did varied, depending on the needs of each person and the events of each day. Right now, he was quietly washing the sores on the feet of an old African man who had traveled for miles with nothing on but a loin cloth, and nothing to his name but a bag with a cup and a handful of rice in it. His feet were rough and bleeding. Brother Randy Joe had carefully sponged the leathery, wound-covered feet with clean water before applying an antibiotic cream.

After the Bible disappeared, he kept losing revenue and eventually lost his cable program. But then he had felt a calling—a calling to live to give, not to get; to preach with actions, not just words. God had met him and changed him totally. He let it all go and answered the call to help the poor in Africa. Brother Randy Joe was still preaching, but now it was preaching with actions as well as words.

When he finished helping the old man, Brother Randy Joe walked back toward his own primitive, cane house. His wife, Arlene, was waiting outside to welcome him home with a kiss. His small children, Randy, Jr. and Rebecca hugged his legs. There was a deep joy in all their hearts.

"Arlene, I jest *lo-o-ve* the *Bi-ible!*"

Author's Afterword

I ask that the readers remember that this is a book of fiction. The aim of the story is to provoke serious thought and discussion about the great gift of the Bible, not to necessarily present my own beliefs on the various issues raised. I am an evangelical pastor. I do believe that Esther is an inspired book of Scripture. I am not endorsing the Apocryha in general, nor the Wisdom of Solomon in particular, as equal to the Word of God. I am a good Protestant regarding the canon.

I mentioned the debate at the Council of Jamnia regarding Esther and the Song of Songs. Most Christians are not aware that Martin Luther, the great German reformer, seriously questioned the canonicity of the book of James. Luther did so because he thought James contradicted Paul on the issue of salvation by faith alone. Luther dubbed James "that right strawy epistle."

Beyond reacting harshly to the ideas presented in Dan Brown's *Da Vinci Code*, have you ever thought about the biblical canon and how it was formed? Many people act as if the Bible "just dropped from the sky," as one of the characters said in the story. The Bible is not a magic book. It came to us from God through people. Scripture has both the pure breath of God in it and the grimy fingerprints of human beings all over it. We must take the complex, even messy, process of the human side of the Bible into account. We would benefit much from taking time to study and gain an understanding about the real human process of formulating the Bible.

The purpose of the Bible does not end with the Bible. An old hymn says, "Beyond the sacred page we seek Thee, Lord." The Bible's purpose is to be used by the Spirit to create a people—the new people of God; to form a people who not only possess a Bible, but who *become a Bible* to the world. The Word is still becoming flesh in the church of Jesus Christ.

I hope you enjoyed the story and I hope that it generates many serious and on-going conversations among those who treasure the Bible. If you feel it has raised more questions for you than it answered, then I have achieved my goal. My greatest hope is that we will read the Bible for the big Story it tells and not use the Bible to belittle, persecute, defame, or reject human beings who bear the marvelous image of God. This hope will be realized when the Church becomes "a message of Christ read by everyone" in the world.

Afterword

The joke's on me. For more than twenty years I have informed my students, often more than once a semester, that I simply have no capacity to read fiction. The story I tell is simple, so let me give it to you now and make it public record. I read two pieces of fiction every year. In mid-December, just after putting the final touches on final exams, I read Charles Dickens' *A Christmas Carol*. In the dog days of summer I read Ernest Hemingway's *The Old Man and the Sea*. Its combination of fishing, which I haven't done in years, and thinking about baseball, which I do all the time, hooks me.

Now I can begin the joke's on me part. I try to read one other piece of fiction every year. I rarely succeed in finishing the book. When one of my former colleagues, an English teacher, raved about a Russian novel, I said to myself, "Self, it's time to read that Russian novel." I lasted about two hundred pages. Which means I got through about a quarter of its endless list of names I couldn't pronounce and eternal train trek across some godforsaken wintry Siberia. The last novel I did get through was Marilynne Robinson's *Gilead*, but the joke was on me again: another colleague told me about the book and I thought it was a biography. Only after I was a hundred pages into the book did I realize it was fiction; the plot fizzled for me from that point on. I made it, but barely.

Then John Frye sent me *Out of Print*. I worried that I wouldn't get through it and would have to confess to him that I hadn't read it. But one morning, before teaching, I started reading it and, much to my surprise, he hooked me. What if the words in our Bibles suddenly disappeared? What would happen to the church if the church had to go on memory? Now, that scared me.

I wonder if this book might not lead us once again to think about what we believe about the Bible. If we are orthodox, we say all the right things about God's Word: inspired; infallible, or inerrant, or at least truth; and we might even bring out the word *authority*. I wonder, though, if we really think those words get the job done. Do they? I don't think so. The point of the Bible is this: God communicates from the Throne of Heaven into the World Way Down Here. What we really believe the most is that the Bible is God's communication with us. But why was it given? This is where *Out of Print* might lead to mini-revivals in our churches today. The Bible is given, not just so we can know God, but also so that the God-who-wants-to-talk-to-us can transform us through that Word. May the book you are now holding remind you of the Bible's divine intent, and may it lead you to treasure that Book's glorious truths so deeply that you become a personal letter from God, written with the invisible ink of God's Spirit.

SCOT MCKNIGHT, PH.D.
Author, *The Jesus Creed*
www.jesuscreed.org

Acknowledgments

I want to thank a community of friends who helped this story get to print. My friend, Dr. Scot McKnight who wrote the kind Afterword, uses the royal or editorial "we" when he talks about the creation of his books. "We" wrote *Jesus Creed*, he contends. He is emphatic that no one writes a book as a solitary soul. I agree with Scot. And, thanks, Scot, for your friendship.

I have an excellent publisher in Tim Beals of Credo Communications. His expert counsel guided me through new publishing territory. Many thanks to Moriah Sharp who helped take the dull edges of my first, amateurish attempt at a fiction story. I am well aware of Moriah's keen eye and profound direction as I read the finished copy. If at any point the story droops, it's traceable directly and only to me.

My friend, Rick Devon of Grey Matter Group, Inc., designed the cover. Cool. Rick, I mean, is very cool as well as the cover design. Thanks, Rick, for your encouraging spirit and generous expertise.

Marie Clark, you are the best! Thanks for donating your time and professional skill on that morning in the city by the river. Your photography is exquisite.

Curt and Karen Howell, thank you for your generous affirmation that helped make this project possible. That you believed in the story and wanted it "out there," deeply encouraged me.

Thanks to all who had to endure hearing bits and pieces of the story as it was coming together: Julie, my wife and friend, and my daughters Leah, Elisha, Lori and Shamar were all instant fans of the concept of the story. They offered many insightful suggestions. Thanks, Shamar, for helping me find a hide out to do some finishing touches on the book.

Ginger Sisson, thank you for the (Orthodox) story about the burial of the Bible with Christ—true or not, it's a great illustration of the One who makes the Word vibrantly alive.

So many others put up with me excitedly telling the story in a nutshell. You know who you are. Brenda and Phil, your delight in the story was like fuel on the fire. Thank you for your enduring friendship.

I want to thank Dr. Phil West, a friend and fellow pastor, for his great insights into the somewhat touchy subject of "open theism." Pastor Phil, with your logical thinking, theological skill, and pastoral heart, you showed me that "open theism" is not something about which to be alarmed, but a stimulating vision of our highly interactive God. While I have only briefly chatted with and e-mail corresponded with Dr. Gregory Boyd, I appreciate him, too, and thank him for his books on "open theism," especially *God at War.*

To my mother, Margaret, to whom I dedicate this book: Thanks, Mom. I love you and I still fondly remember being one of the kids sitting at your feet as you taught the Child Evangelism Fellowship club in our home. You have always loved the Word of God. But even more, you have lived it.

JOHN W. FRYE
Grand Rapids, Michigan
August 2007